A Close Encounter of the Worst Kind

"What's that?" shouts T.O.D.

"You mean you don't know what water is?" you ask. "I thought you were programmed with all kinds of knowledge."

"I am," replies the android. "But I wasn't referring to water. That's made up of hydrogen and oxygen. I was referring to those aliens who have just surrounded us."

"Aliens!" you shout, looking up. A dozen blue globe-shaped vehicles are floating in the air around you.

One of the ships dives down and zooms over your head. A green ray shoots out.

WHOMP!

EXPLORER™

Adventure on the Frontiers of Science.

#4

ESCAPE FROM JUPITER

Seth McEvoy

Illustrated by
Walter P. Martishius

A Byron Preiss Visual Publications, Inc., Book

Scholastic Inc.

New York Toronto London Auckland Sydney

Special thanks to Jean Feiwel, Greg Holch, Regina Griffin, and Bruce Stevenson.

Book design by Alex Jay
Cover painting by Bob Eggleton
Cover design by Alex Jay
Mechanicals by Mary LeCleir

Editor: Ruth Ashby

THE COUNTDOWN BEGINS...

You are an explorer. You journey to places no one has ever been and face dangers no one has ever known.

Now you have a new assignment. In a moment you'll be given a briefing and will meet some of the other members of your team. At your disposal you will have the latest in scientific knowledge and technology.

Despite these advantages, at times you and your team may be exposed to extreme peril. Only the decisions you make will enable you to survive.

Are you willing to accept the risks? The choice is up to you.

■ *When you're ready, turn the page.*

PROJECT SUMMARY

Your assignment: You must explore the moons of Jupiter to see if they can supply enough air, water, and energy for Earth's future needs.

By the year 2025, Earth is dangerously overcrowded. Fifty billion people live on the planet, and millions more are born each day. The air and water are hopelessly polluted; there's not enough food; and our coal, gas, and oil are nearly gone.

Earth's resources are almost used up. But what about nearby planets? Can humans live there and build space colonies?

Mercury and Venus are uninhabitable because they're too hot, Mars is nearly as barren as our Moon, and the planets beyond Jupiter are too cold to sustain human life.

Jupiter is also uninhabitable because it is only a gigantic mass of compressed gases. Any spaceship trying to land on Jupiter would be crushed by the deadly heat and pressure of its thick atmosphere.

Jupiter's moons may be our only hope. They are about the right size and may contain vital elements that can sustain human life.

You will accompany the first manned mission to the moons of Jupiter. If you can find air, water, and fuel, you will be able to save the human race.

■ *The following Personnel Dossiers and Equipment Report contain orientation material that will help you on your mission to the moons of Jupiter. If you prefer to board your spacecraft now, turn to page 1.*

PERSONNEL DOSSIERS

GEORGE SPIRO, Mission Commander

Born: January 27, 1995; Athens, Greece

Education: B.S.E.E., Lakeport Technical Institute, 2017; Ph.D., Geneva University, 2019

Credits: Test Pilot, Rugg Aerospace Industries, 2015–2017 (while an undergraduate student in engineering); professor, Astronomy Department, Leningrad Academy 2020–2022; winner of the Burgess Astronomy Prize 2022; Editor, *Space Today* magazine, 2022–2023; Chief Pilot, International Space Agency, Peru, 2022–present (Co-commander of ISA Mission to asteroid belt, 2024).

Remarks: Mr. Spiro is a highly qualified astronaut as well as one of the world's leading amateur experts on the planet Jupiter. George Spiro is highly intelligent, physically fit, and able to endure physical and emotional stress better than most human beings. However, his fellow test pilots have nicknamed him "Mr. Freeze" because he seems cold and unemotional even when he's not piloting a spaceship.

PERSONNEL DOSSIERS

DR. REGINALD GRANVILLE, Physicist

Born: August 3, 1989; Beaconsfield, England

Education: Ph.D., Surrey Institute of Technology, 2010

Credits: Chairman, Physics Department, Glasgow Technological University, Scotland, 2015–2020; chief research scientist, International Space Agency, 2021–present; winner of the Bolton Prize 2014; A. L. Zagat Fellowship 2017; and Rhinebeck Chair in Physics 2020; author of 317 scientific papers; chairman, Bergey Conference on Jupiter, 2023.

Remarks: Dr. Granville has made the planet Jupiter his life's work. An advanced student at an early age, he was able to complete his doctorate (on "Jupiter as a Space Colony") by the age of twenty-one. He often jokes around, but he's very serious when it comes to Jupiter and its moons. Even though he is somewhat single-minded and eccentric, he can be relied upon to solve almost any kind of problem.

PERSONNEL DOSSIERS

T.O.D.; Transplanetary Omnitronic Droid

Created: 2024, DataTech Computers, Android Division

Remarks: T.O.D. is an android, created by Dr. Timothy Huang (see Explorer #2). T.O.D. has the ability to think and act like a human, but he does not need food, water, or air to survive and is powered by a micro-miniature fusion reactor in his chest. T.O.D. uses computer circuitry that attempts to mimic the thought processes of the human brain. This produces responses that are useful, but occasionally results in unique, unpredictable, or humorous interactions.

EQUIPMENT REPORT

THUNDERBOLT: A multi-stage inter-planetary rocket with a top speed of 31,000 miles per hour. It was designed by the International Space Agency for a four-year, round-trip voyage to the moons of Jupiter. The crew will consist of a pilot, a scientist, an observer, and a robot.

TERRA-TRAK CRAWLER: A two-person vehicle capable of maneuvering over sand, rock, ice, or snow. It has an air-tight enclosed cab, rechargeable batteries, and uses three gripper treads that can climb over almost any surface.

SONAREST CHAMBER: A capsule in which a human body is frozen for long voyages through space. The life processes are suspended so that no food, water, or oxygen is consumed.

■ *End orientation material. If you want more information about Jupiter and its moons, turn to page 114.*

■ *If you are ready to begin your assignment now, turn to page 1.*

You race down the steps of the sleek white International Space Agency jet. Shielding your eyes from the bright noonday sun, you see a tall blue rocket on the runway ahead of you. Five smaller rockets are lined up behind it.

A gray-haired man with a thick mustache rushes up to greet you. "I'm Dr. Reginald Granville," he says in a British accent. "Welcome to Quito, Ecuador, land of rich Inca tradition, poor cups of tea, and the ISA Launching Pad. I'm the science officer and best card player on the Jupiter mission. You'll meet our other two companions in a few moments."

He shakes your hand vigorously, then picks up your bag and starts walking toward the large blue rocket. "Let's get ready for takeoff."

"Hey, wait," you yell. "I was told we weren't leaving until next week!"

"I thought they informed you," says Dr. Granville. "Takeoff has been pushed up to this afternoon. You won't even have time to meet Ms. Fowler, the ISA president. I hope the change in plans won't be too much of an inconvenience, old bean."

"Why are we leaving so soon?"

"Because I want to return to Earth in

time to do my Christmas shopping," he says with a mischievous grin. "No, seriously, we really *do* have to take off almost immediately."

"What happened?"

"The ISA astronomers sighted a deadly meteor shower that would cross our flight path if we left next week. It would make the *Thunderbolt* look like a giant Swiss cheese. By the way, do you like Swiss cheese?"

"Sure I like it, but what's the *Thunderbolt*? Our spaceship?"

"Of course," he replies. "You didn't think it was a submarine sandwich, did you?"

Before you can answer, he continues talking: "I'm glad to hear you like Swiss cheese. I've packed quite a bit for our trip. It's one of my favorite foods, even more than chocolate cream pie. But I won't be bringing much of that on this voyage."

"Glad to hear it," you reply.

"Now step right this way," says the scientist. "We've got a four-year journey ahead of us, so let's get started."

The two of you swiftly cross the pavement. Three technicians are making last-minute changes on the gigantic rocket as you approach. You climb up a short ladder and ride an open cage elevator to the top of a narrow platform that surrounds the blue spaceship.

"You can get a better view of the city of Quito from up here," says Dr. Granville. "We picked Ecuador as our ISA launching site because it's two miles above sea level."

"What's the advantage of that?" you ask.

"We don't run the risk of being attacked by sea monsters," he answers with a wink.

"Are there any *other* reasons?" you reply.

"Yes," the scientist says. "By being two miles in the air, we need less fuel to propel us out of Earth's gravity."

"That sounds reasonable."

"Very reasonable! When we're planning a four-year trip, we don't want to waste one drop of fuel."

You then take a long look at the surrounding countryside. "A four-year journey," you mutter.

"You aren't worried about this expedition, are you?" asks Dr. Granville.

"Of course not," you reply confidently. "I wouldn't have entered the Space Lottery if I hadn't wanted to be one of the first people to go see the moons of Jupiter."

"I'm afraid this isn't going to be much of a sight-seeing vacation," the scientist reminds you. "We'll have much work to do."

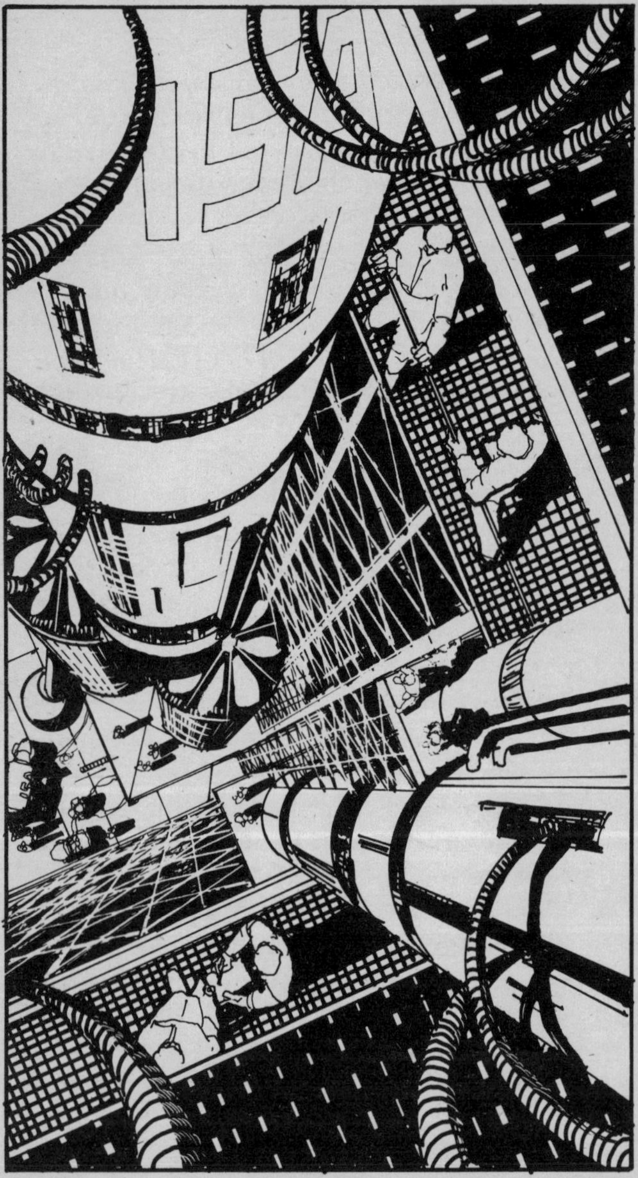

"I realize that," you answer. "I know how important it is that we find out if the moons of Jupiter have the resources humans will need in order to survive in space."

"Glad to hear you say that," says Dr. Granville. "The Space Lottery is quite a jolly good idea, if I do say so myself. So many people bought a ticket that we were able to finance this expedition without any government assistance."

"I guess I'm pretty lucky I get to go on this mission."

He shakes his head from side to side. "Luck made you one of the fifty finalists. We picked you to accompany us because we needed someone with your outstanding strength, courage, and intelligence. You may not realize it, but you scored higher on the Interstellar Training Test than many of our own scientists."

Suddenly you hear a loud buzzer, and the technicians scurry away from the base of the rocket.

"Where are they going?" you ask.

Dr. Granville glances at his watch. "The final countdown is about to begin. And if we don't get inside right now, the pilot may leave without us."

■ *Enter the* Thunderbolt *rocket by turning to page 12.*

When you open your eyes, you see a three-eyed silver ball talking to you through a thick plastic window. Everything in your mind is hazy, and it takes you a second to remember where you are.

"Wake up," says T.O.D.

"I'm sleepy," you reply, turning over. "Give me another hour."

The android's round head snakes over the top of the Sonarest chamber and its face peers into yours. "You must wake up now," it says. "There's trouble and we need your help."

You stretch your arms and legs. You feel stiff and weary. T.O.D. opens the chamber's lid, and you bump against it and remember that you're beyond the pull of gravity.

"Where are we, anyway?" you ask.

"We're very near Jupiter's outermost moon, Sinope," the android replies.

"So what's the problem?"

"Mr. Spiro tried to smash us into it," it explains.

"That's right, old bean," says Dr. Granville, in his thick British accent. "If T.O.D. hadn't grabbed George when he did, we'd all be mashed potatoes by now."

Holding on to the side of the chamber, you ask, "I don't understand. Why did he try to kill us?"

"Who can understand humans?" T.O.D. answers.

"Certainly not you," snaps Dr. Granville. "Anyway, Spiro says that he wanted us to die, so we'd be famous space heros, who were so brave they gave their lives in an attempt to save Earth."

"But won't we be famous when we discover new resources on Jupiter's moons?" you ask.

"Apparently Spiro was afraid we wouldn't find anything," Dr. Granville explains. "I always thought he was a bit cracked in the old noodle."

"Where is he now?"

"T.O.D. locked him in one of the storage cabins below," says the scientist.

"Mr. Spiro wants to talk to you," the android says.

"I wouldn't bother, if I were you," Dr. Granville says. "He's a raving lunatic, and he might be dangerous."

"But then who will fly the ship?" you ask.

"You will," says Dr. Granville. "I'll be too busy calculating our course trajectories and thrust ratios."

"Why not let me pilot the ship?" asks the android.

"Because I don't trust machines," he replies. "Especially after you nearly poisoned me on the last mission by trying to make orange juice from paint thinner and orange food coloring. No, only a human can have the reflexes and precision that's needed to land this spacecraft."

"But I've never flown a rocket before," you say.

"Nothing to it," Dr. Granville explains. "Most of it is controlled by computers. It's very similar to a video game. T.O.D. will show you the procedure."

"I can do it," you reply confidently.

"Wait," says T.O.D. "I can play video games, too!"

"Bah! You *are* a video game, you bucket of bolts," grumbles Dr. Granville. "But I wouldn't waste a quarter on you." Turning to you, he says, "We'd better get topside and make sure we're on course."

"But Mr. Spiro said he wants to talk to our friend here," reminds T.O.D.

"So what?" Dr. Granville replies. "He's just a raving lunatic. But I'll let our new pilot make up his own mind."

■ *Do you want to ignore Mr. Spiro and start learning to fly the ship now? Turn to page 28.*

■ *Do you want to talk to Mr. Spiro and see what he wants? Turn to page 32.*

"I'd like to learn all I can," you say. "Dr. Granville mentioned that Mr. Spiro thought he'd found a new moon of Jupiter. How many moons are there?"

The android stares at you with his big round glowing eyes and answers, "Sixteen. But only four are large enough to possibly contain resources to supply Earth's future needs or support a space colony. The rest are just small bits of rock."

"So tell me about these four moons. How big are they?"

"About the size of Earth's Moon or the planet Mercury."

"What are they like?"

"Each of the four moons is very different."

"How?"

"The innermost of the four largest moons is called Io. It's the most bizarre moon in the solar system and is bright orange, red, yellow, and black."

"What's it made out of — pizza?"

"Not quite. Experts believe that Io is made up of sulfur and related compounds."

"I bet it doesn't smell very good."

"I wouldn't know, not being able to smell. The planet is riddled with active volcanoes that throw molten sulfur three hundred kilometers into the air. Its volcanic heat could generate enough energy to run a million factories."

"We'll have to be careful about that one," you say. "What about the others?"

"Europa, which is the next satellite out from Io, appears to have lots and lots of ice. The whole moon is covered with a very thick layer of smooth ice. Europa could supply enough pure water to satisfy the thirst of every plant, animal, and human being."

"Europa sounds like fun," you reply. "I should have brought my ice skates."

"If you like winter sports, then you'll love the next moon. Ganymede is believed to be covered with patches of rock and a variety of different kinds of ices."

"What do you mean, a variety? Ice is ice, isn't it?"

"No," the android replies. "Ice is *any* frozen liquid. Scientists think Ganymede has ice made up of frozen ammonia, methane, and other frozen gases and liquids."

"What are ammonia and methane?"

"They are basic chemicals that can be used to make things that humans need, such as fuel, fertilizers, and other useful products."

"What's the fourth big moon all about?" you ask.

"Callisto is covered with craters and looks like Earth's Moon, but unlike our Moon, Callisto is made up of water and soil frozen together."

"Like a giant mudball?"

"Yes, but no one knows for sure. That's the whole point. Instruments and theories can only tell so much. Our mission is to bring back samples from each of the four largest moons."

"I can hardly wait," you say.

"You won't *have* to wait once you get into the Sonarest chamber," says the android.

■ *To begin your two-year nap, turn to page 18.*

You duck your head and climb into the central cabin of the spacecraft. Inside you see three green padded chairs. Every inch of the walls is covered with video screens, push buttons, dials, and levers.

"Boy, would I love to get my hands on those controls," you say. "But I guess it would take a genius to figure out how to fly this thing."

"That's right," says a thin man with red hair. "That's me and that's what I'm here for. You're just along for the ride. So I would appreciate it if you would not do anything to interfere with my work."

"George Spiro, you're being frightfully rude and very unfair," says Dr. Granville sternly. "You're just angry because our friend here received a higher score than you did on the training program. Besides, if it hadn't been for all those Space Lottery ticket buyers, you wouldn't be going to Jupiter at all."

"Tickets!" Mr. Spiro grumbles. "I think it's terrible that the only way we can finance an expedition is by selling tickets

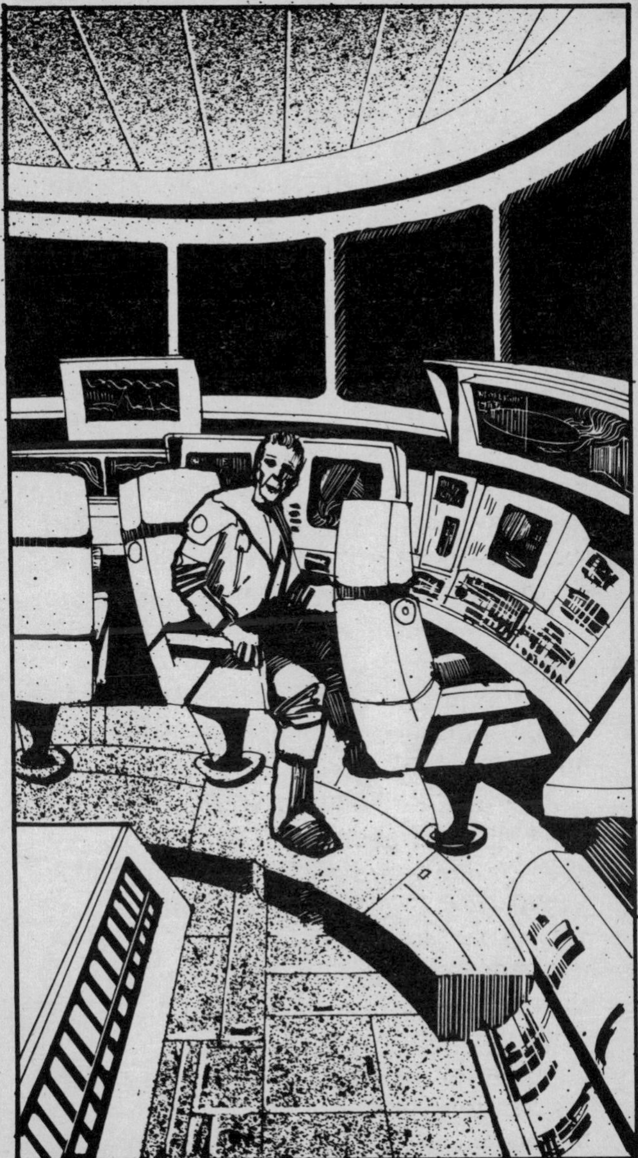

to thrill seekers! If we don't find new resources in space, this overcrowded planet of ours won't survive another decade."

"I want to help, too," you tell him. "That's why I bought a ticket — I never believed I'd actually win and get to go to Jupiter."

"Well, you're not going if you don't strap yourself in," Mr. Spiro says angrily. "Takeoff is in five minutes."

"Don't pay attention to George," whispers Dr. Granville. "He just likes to criticize and complain. He gets my vote for President of the Interplanetary Complainers League. But don't worry about him, he doesn't mean you any harm, old chum. Pick a chair and make yourself comfortable."

You climb into one of the soft, padded chairs and carefully buckle your three seat belts. You have one for your chest, one for your waist, and one for your legs.

"Just remember," says Mr. Spiro. "I'm the mission commander. Your life, and *all* of our lives may depend on doing exactly *what* I say, *when* I say."

"You can count on me," you eagerly reply. "I'll try to help any way I can."

You examine the cabin more closely. "I thought there were four of us going on the trip," you say.

"No, only three," says Spiro. "I'm the

pilot, Dr. Granville is the scientist, and you're the observer. What gave you the idea that four people were going?"

"Dr. Granville did," you answer.

"Not quite," the scientist replies. "I said there were two more *companions*, but T.O.D. isn't a human. He's a cross between a pocket calculator and a very annoying chimpanzee."

"That's your opinion," says a new voice from behind you. Even though you try to turn, your seat belts prevent you from twisting your head around to see who's speaking.

"T.O.D., get below," orders Mr. Spiro.

"But I wanted to say hello to Dr. Granville and meet our new passenger!"

Suddenly you see a round silver shape zoom in front of your face. It looks like a shiny metal basketball with dials, switches, and three big black spots. "Hi," it says. "I'm T.O.D."

You notice a long skinny neck attaching the sphere to a tubular metal body. "Uh, hi," you reply, giving your name. "What's your last name, T.O.D.?"

"Droid."

"T.O.D. Droid?"

"No!" says the head as it gazes at you with its three dark glowing eyes. "T.O.D. stands for Transplanetary Omnitronic 'Droid."

"Then you're a robot!"

"Sort of, but I'm *better* than a robot," it says proudly. "I can think and sing and play Parcheesi. And I can do this. Can you?"

It loops its head around and ties its neck in a knot.

"No," you reply, trying not to laugh. "But I wouldn't want to, either."

"T.O.D., go below instantly!" snaps Spiro.

"I can't do that," says the android.

"Why not?"

"Because it will take two point three seconds to go below, and instantly is a shorter time period than that."

"All right," Spiro says firmly. "Go below and secure yourself."

"You bet," the android replies. It unties the knot in its neck. As it rolls away, you now can see that its silver tube-shaped body has two arms on each side and rolls on small wheels at its base.

"Beastly contraption," mutters Dr. Granville. "I wish it wasn't going with us."

"Why?" you ask. "Don't you like robots?"

"No," he replies. "They're a complete waste of perfectly good metal. A dozen toasters could have been made out of him with enough room left over for a cigarette lighter!"

"He seems harmless enough to me," you say.

"Harmless!" sputters Dr. Granville. "On our last mission, that rotten robot erased all my Martian music tapes, mixed up the data in my alien address book, and put horseradish in my peanut butter and Swiss cheese sandwich. And besides, he cheats at Parcheesi!"

"Now let's be quiet," Spiro shouts angrily. "We're about to lift off."

"Yes, teacher," jokes Dr. Granville.

Ignoring his remark, Spiro asks, "Is everyone ready for takeoff?"

"I'm ready," you say, gripping the sides of your chair.

"Wait! I forgot my long underwear!" jokes Dr. Granville.

"Too late," replies the pilot as he presses a button. You hear a loud roaring from below. The whole ship starts to shake!

■ *Rocket into space by turning to page 19.*

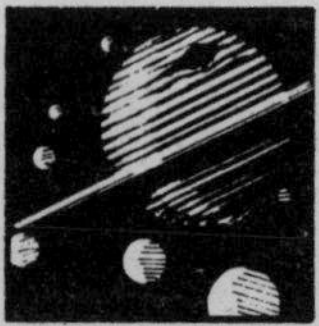

T.O.D. helps you float into the green Sonarest chamber. He shuts the thick plastic door. You lie back quietly and listen to the sound of your own breathing.

You hear a hissing sound. Cold air rushes in around your body.

Looking through the plastic door, you see T.O.D. float through the cabin. Your eyelids get heavy and you can't keep them open.

Your last thought is that you wish you had a blanket.

Then you fall asleep.

■ *When you're ready to wake up, turn to page 6.*

As the ship vibrates, you feel as if a ten-ton elephant just sat on your chest. The rocket engines roar, and you grip the sides of your chair as you blast into space.

Seconds go by slowly. You wonder if you'll ever be able to breathe freely again. The video screens on the wall ahead of you are just a blaze of light. Then you hear a loud explosion!

"What was that?" you manage to mumble, even though the gravity forces are nearly tearing your teeth out.

"Just the first stage of the rocket breaking free," Spiro answers. "The *Thunderbolt* is a three-stage rocket. The first two stages are used just to get us out of the grip of Earth's gravity."

BLAM!

You hear a second explosion.

"That's stage two," he adds. "Right on schedule. We'll be in free fall in two minutes."

The engine becomes quieter. The video screen goes black. As your eyes adjust, you see stars beginning to appear on the darkened screen that hangs above your head.

"We're in space!" you exclaim.

"That's right," says Dr. Granville. "The video screen was temporarily blanked out by the tremendous blast of ions as we shot up through the atmosphere."

Mr. Spiro carefully checks all the meters and adjusts some of the dials. "We're on course," he announces.

"You can unfasten your safety belts," says Dr. Granville.

Unbuckling the three belts that hold you to the chair, you stretch your body . . . and suddenly float up into the room.

"Hey!" you yell. "What happened?"

"I warned you we'd be in free fall," Spiro grumbles. "You'll be weightless for the next two years."

"Does that mean I can eat all I want and not gain weight?" asks Dr. Granville with a wink.

"Of course not," the pilot angrily replies. "But you must learn how to get around without the help of gravity. It's like swimming."

You wave your arms and legs in the air. Wriggling around, you manage to get back to your seat.

"This will take some getting used to," you say. "It's a lot harder than it was in the training simulator."

"Don't worry," says Dr. Granville. "We're going to sleep through most of the trip. We'll save food, water, and air that way. If we didn't go into suspended animation, we'd need to carry a lot more supplies. It would take a hundred rocket ships to hold it all."

"Speaking of which," says Spiro, "we should get in our Sonarest chambers without further delay."

"What's your hurry?" asks Dr. Granville. "I thought we could play a game of cards first."

"No, thank you," Spiro replies coldly. He expertly dives through the hatch and disappears from sight.

"He's not much fun," Dr. Granville says to you. "I don't think he likes me."

"Why is that?" you ask.

"Because he thought he had discovered a new moon of Jupiter two years ago. But he was wrong."

"What's that got to do with you?"

Dr. Granville sighs. "I was the one who proved he was wrong. We had a terrible argument about it at the Bergey Jupiter Conference, and he's never forgiven me. He thinks he's the world's living expert on Jupiter."

"I thought you were!" you say. "I remember *Newsbeat* magazine calling you that in an article last year."

"Well, George Spiro doesn't think so," the scientist replies. "*He* thinks *he* knows it all."

T.O.D. pops his metal head up through the hatch. "Spiro told me to tell you to get into the Sonarest chambers."

"Nag, nag, nag," grumbles Dr. Granville. "We're coming."

Dr. Granville gets up out of his chair and bounces up to the ceiling and bangs his head. "Ouch! This sure isn't as easy as it looks."

"Are you hurt?" you ask.

"Of course not," he replies. "My head's harder than a banker's heart." You watch as he struggles through the hatch.

You float up into the air and kick out at the wall. Zoom! You shoot through the hatch and enter the lower cabin.

Just before you crash into the floor, T.O.D. grabs you with his four arms.

"Thanks," you say. "Where are Dr. Granville and Mr. Spiro?"

"They're in their own Sonarest chambers," the android replies. It points to two green tubes set into the wall. You can see dim human outlines inside.

Brrr. You shiver. "Are you sure it's safe?" you ask as T.O.D. leads you to the third Sonarest chamber.

"How would I know?" says the android. "I'm not getting in one!"

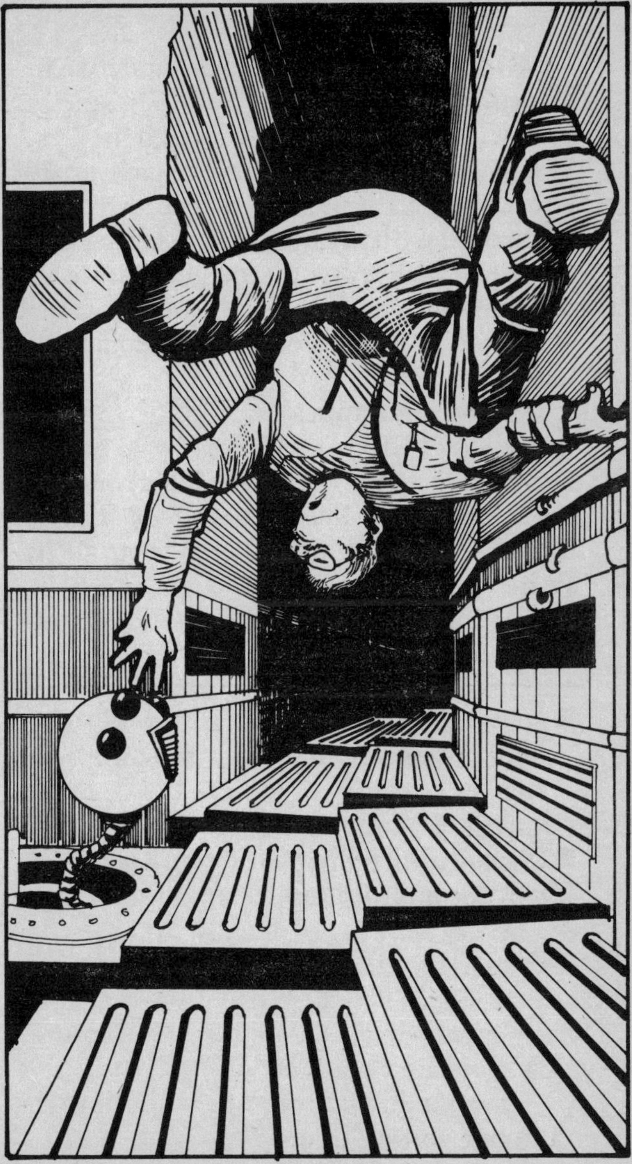

"What are you going to do while we're asleep?"

"Just sit around and wait," it replies. "I'll wake up Spiro if there're any problems. Maybe I'll paint a picture. Or play basketball with my head. I suppose I could reread all the Jupiter data tapes that we've brought with us. Or take a look at Dr. Granville's new files on asteroid soup recipes."

"Jupiter data tapes?"

"Yes," says T.O.D. "I have files of everything that's ever been recorded about Jupiter. Would you like me to tell you a little bit more about Jupiter before you go to sleep?"

You think for a moment and tell the android your answer.

■ *If you'd like T.O.D. to give you some information about Jupiter now, turn to page 9.*

■ *If you'd like to enter the Sonarest chamber now, turn to page 18.*

"What's that flashing light?" you ask as you strap yourself in the pilot's chair. "Have we run out of fuel or water?"

"I don't know," says Dr. Granville. "I'm an expert on Jupiter, not rockets. For all I know, that's the alarm that tells us that our toast is done."

T.O.D. floats up beside you. One of his shiny arms points toward the flashing red light. "You probably want to know what that is," he says.

"Yes, it might be helpful," you reply. "It could mean we're in *serious* trouble."

"Do you want me to tell you what it is?"

"YES!"

"All right, I'll tell you."

You turn to Dr. Granville and make a face. "Is it against the law to strangle robots?"

"Probably not. Anyway, T.O.D., do tell us what the flashing light indicates."

"It's telling us that the *Thunderbolt* is about to crash into a large object. From the size of it, I'd say that we're about to be flattened by Callisto."

"Oh, no!" you exclaim. "What do we do?"

"You have two options," says T.O.D.

"Tell me what they are," you order.

"One: You can try to land on Callisto. Two: You can try to avoid crashing into it."

"Which should I do?" you ask Dr. Granville.

The scientist shakes his head. "I don't know. Callisto is the least likely of the four large moons to contain the materials we could use to manufacture the air, water, or fuel that we need so desperately."

"You don't really need much water," says T.O.D. "Mr. Spiro didn't destroy the food supplies and in them are contained enough juices, sodas, and other liquids to meet your needs."

Dr. Granville shakes his head. "We need water to manufacture our air," he explains.

"May I give my opinion?" T.O.D. asks.

"Yes."

"You might want to land on Callisto, even though it won't provide the materials you want. If you land now, you can take the time to consider carefully all your options and plan what you want to do next."

"That's a good point," you say.

"Decide quickly, old bean," Dr. Granville urges. "I don't want to become a human pancake."

"What kind of pancake do you want to become?" asks T.O.D.

You think fast.

■ *Do you want to avoid Callisto? Turn to page 40.*

■ *Do you want to land on Callisto? Turn to page 37.*

"It doesn't matter what he has to say," you say. "There's so much to learn about piloting that I'd better do it now."

Flexing your muscles, you step back, take a leap, and glide through the hatch to the control room above your head. You're getting better at this all the time!

You strap yourself into the control chair. The dials and switches are all labeled, but there seem to be a million of them.

T.O.D. starts explaining what each button does while Dr. Granville calculates your current position. The video screen above your head shows the giant planet of Jupiter, looking like a huge striped beach ball. You see a couple of tiny moons nearby, orbiting around their parent world. In the background are thousands of bright stars in all the colors of the rainbow.

"This button will control our thruster rockets. The acceleration rate is that dial there and the actual speed is. . . ."

Your head swims with all the new information. Your stomach starts to growl. "When do we eat?" you ask.

"I don't eat at all," T.O.D. replies.

"I know that," you say. "But when do Dr. Granville and I eat?"

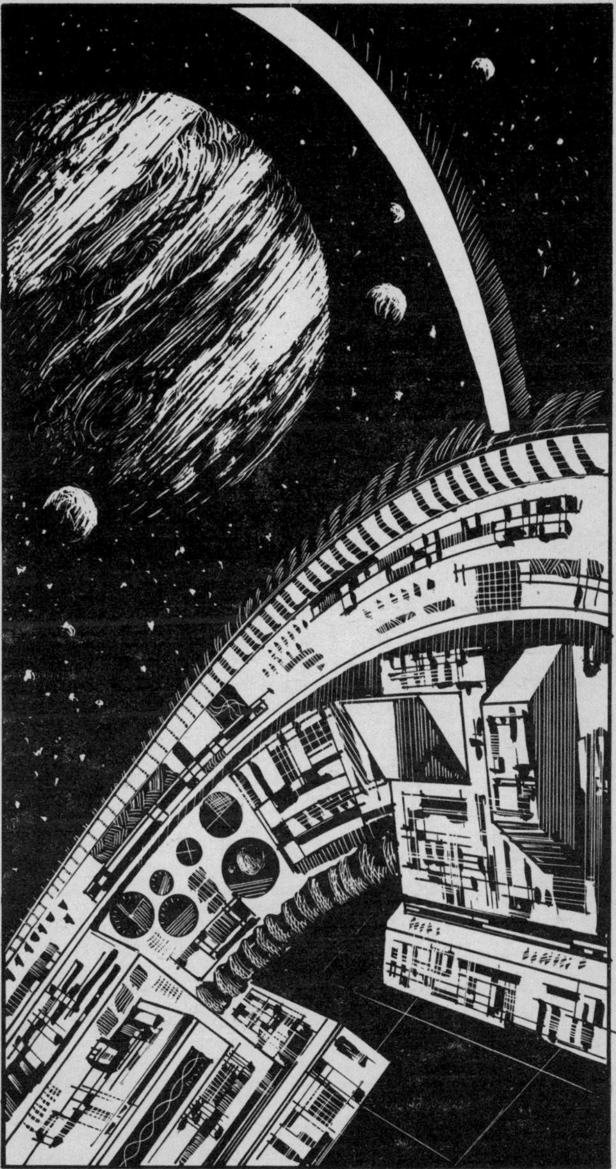

"Whenever you put food into your mouths," the android continues.

You sigh with exasperation. "All right, who prepares our food?"

"I do, whenever you ask me. Would you like some now?"

You nod your head eagerly.

"Don't forget to feed Mr. Spiro," says Dr. Granville, looking up from his computer. "Even though he tried to kill us, we must take him back to Earth for a trial. And don't poison him, either! Your cooking is a menace to the human race."

The android disappears down the hatch. You continue studying the control panel, until you suddenly feel so dizzy from hunger that you rest your head on your arm.

"I say, do you feel sleepy?" Dr. Granville asks, letting out a loud yawn.

"Yes," you reply. "But we've slept for two years already."

Suddenly T.O.D. shoots up out of the hatch. "Mr. Spiro is gone."

"What?" you shout.

"Mr. Spiro is gone," the robot repeats.

"But where could he go?" asks Dr. Granville. "It's not as if he could jump out of the ship."

"That's just what he did," explains T.O.D. "He broke out of the cabin, and I noticed that the air lock is open on the outside door."

"I guess he didn't want to face a trial back on Earth," you say.

"He obviously didn't want to face us again, either. He must have realized he could never take control of the ship," says Dr. Granville. "Oh, well, I guess that's more air, food, water, and fuel for us."

"Not exactly," T.O.D. informs you. "Before Mr. Spiro left the ship, he opened the main valve of the air tank. You have only enough oxygen to breathe for the next few hours."

"So that's why we feel so sleepy," says Dr. Granville.

"Wait," says the android, "I haven't finished my report."

"What else did Mr. Spiro do?" you ask. "What else *could* he do?"

"Perhaps he did you a favor," T.O.D. explains. "Dying of oxygen starvation is not supposed to be pleasant, from my analysis of human physiology."

"What else?" orders Dr. Granville. "Come on, you rust-eating robot, get to the point."

"Mr. Spiro jammed the rocket fuel controllers wide open. The motors should explode about — "

KABOOM!

THE END

"I think I'd better talk to Mr. Spiro before I do anything else," you say. "Perhaps T.O.D. misunderstood what was happening."

"I know what I saw," says the robot, "and I'm sure that Mr. Spiro was trying to destroy our ship."

"Just the same," you reply, "I'd feel more comfortable hearing his explanation."

"Don't bother," Dr. Granville says. "Even though I don't much care for this little android, he's not capable of telling a lie."

"T.O.D.," you say. "Take me to the prisoner."

The android reaches out and grabs you by the arm and yanks you forward.

"NO!" you shout. "*Lead* me to the prisoner."

"Sorry," T.O.D. replies. "You said to *take* you, and I am programmed to follow orders."

Dr. Granville chuckles. "See what I mean? He makes a great video tape recorder, but a very poor butler."

"Lead on, T.O.D.," you say.

"I'll stay up here," replies the scientist.

You follow T.O.D. through a hatch to the floor below.

But as you enter the lowest of the three main cabins, you see Mr. Spiro floating in one corner.

"I thought you were supposed to be locked up!" you say.

"I was," replies the crazed pilot. "But I broke out, and now I'm going to finish destroying this mission. I'll finally get my revenge against Dr. Granville. He stopped me from becoming a world class scientist and getting the recognition I deserved."

"T.O.D., lock him up again," you order.

"Don't come near me, robot!"

"Dr. Granville told me not to follow your orders any longer, Mr. Spiro," explains the android, as it begins to swim through the air toward the pilot.

"I'm not ordering you, then, I'm informing you that I'll turn this valve and let all the fuel and water drain into space."

"You've already started to drain the air tanks, I see," says the android. "I must stop you before you do any more damage!"

Mr. Spiro twists the valve!

T.O.D. leaps through space.

You dive through the air right behind him.

Spiro dodges, and T.O.D. crashes into the wall.

"I'll grab him!" you shout, lunging after him.

T.O.D.'s arms slash through the air and catch Spiro's shirt. The cloth rips, and he gets away.

You slam into the pilot's back and knock him back toward the android.

"Hurry!" you yell. "We've got to get to the air valve!"

The android pins Mr. Spiro to the wall. You fly over them and twist the heavy valve back to its normal position.

"You're too late, robot," snarls Mr. Spiro.

At that moment, Dr. Granville floats down from the cabin above. "What's all this noise? I thought the low gravity aerobics lessons didn't start until *next* week."

"You'll be doing aerobics in heaven pretty soon," Mr. Spiro exclaims. "I've finally gotten my revenge on you, Granville. I emptied all the air, water, and fuel storage tanks. You'll soon be DEAD!"

The scientist scans the dials on the wall. "Not quite," he says. "Fortunately, the food and drink supplies are untouched, and we've still got enough fuel, air, and water for a day or two."

"But it will take two years to get back to Earth!" you exclaim.

"He's right," agrees the android. "Even with the Sonarest chambers, you won't

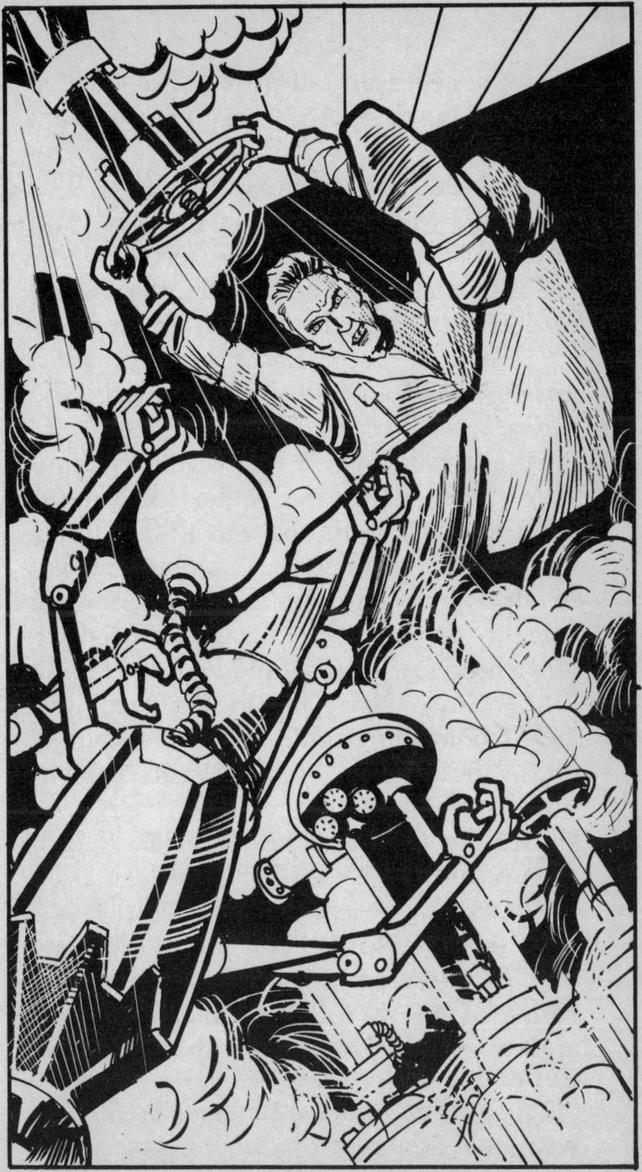

have the necessary air or water to survive such a long trip. And there isn't enough fuel anyway."

"See, see!" Spiro shouts gleefully. "I've managed to destroy your mission, and now we'll all be worldwide heros."

"You won't be a hero!" you reply. "We'll radio Earth and tell them all about you."

"I took care of that first," the pilot answers with an evil grin. "I smashed the radio."

"We're not finished yet," says Dr. Granville. "We've got the moons of Jupiter right here. Our mission was to find out if the moons contained the resources needed to support human life. If our theories are correct, the basic chemicals we need for air, water, and fuel should be right here."

Mr. Spiro struggles to get free, but T.O.D. holds him tightly. "You're the crazy ones," he shouts, "not me. You'll never find anything on those moons!"

"We'll soon see about that," Dr. Granville replies.

"Then let's get started!" you reply.

"That's the spirit," Dr. Granville says. "We'd better get upstairs and plot our course of action. T.O.D., lock up Mr. Spiro and make sure he can't escape again."

■ *Float up to the control room by turning to page 25.*

"We're going to land rather hard," says Dr. Granville.

T.O.D. tells you the procedure. Your stomach turns over as you adjust the dial for landing.

You watch as the crater-filled moon appears on the rearview video screen. Your fingers grip the chair tightly, and you count off the seconds until touchdown.

WHAM!

Your seat belts stop you from being thrown out of your chair. "I think we made it in one piece," you say.

"The air in here seems all right," reports Dr. Granville. "My biggest worry was that the force of the landing would crack open the *Thunderbolt* like an overripe melon."

"My head seems to have been hurt," says T.O.D. "I can't move my neck."

You turn and see the robot's head in a corner of the cabin. Its body is in another corner.

Dr. Granville unstraps his seat belt, rushes over to the robot, and picks up its head. "Alas, poor T.O.D., I knew him well," he says as he holds up the head.

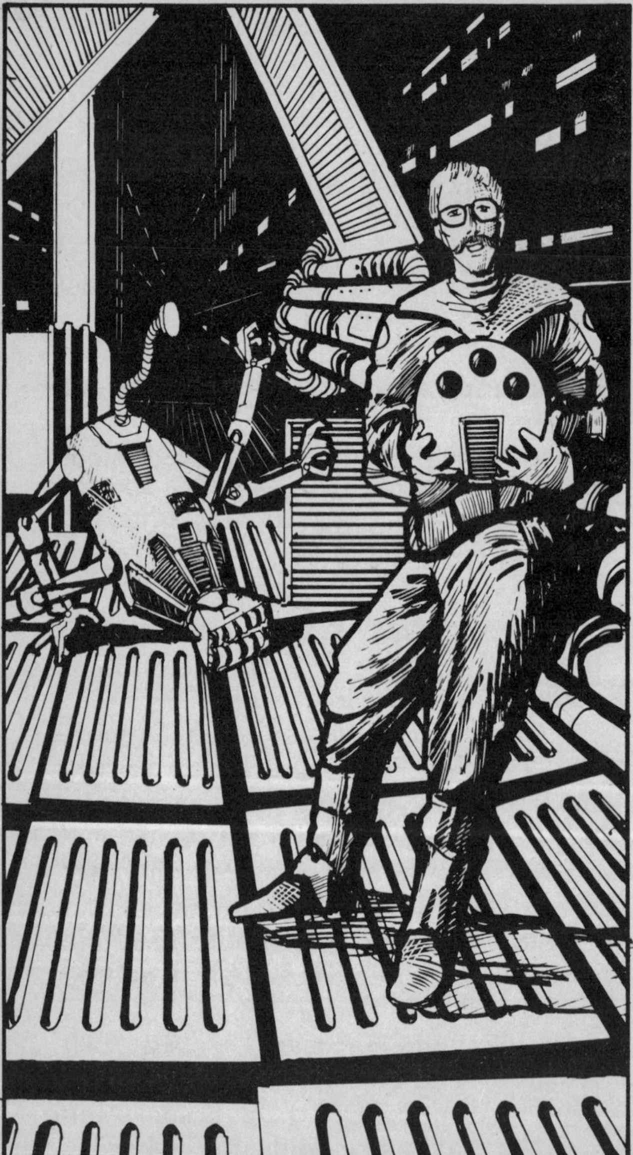

"Quit misquoting Shakespeare," T.O.D.'s head grumbles. "Can you attach my head back to my body? It must have shaken loose when we plowed into Callisto."

"Even if I could," replies the scientist, "I don't think I want to."

"What a nasty man," says T.O.D.

"I'm sure Dr. Granville was just kidding," you say. "He knows that we need you to help out."

"For what, pray tell?" grumbles Dr. Granville as he reattaches T.O.D.'s head. "This robot is no more useful than an encyclopedia. And it's a lot noisier."

"At least I don't use up air, food, and water," replies the android, swiveling his head around.

You sigh. "Don't remind us that we're living on borrowed time." Turning to Dr. Granville, you say, "Now that we've landed on Callisto, what are we going to do about our predicament?"

"We have two problems to solve," begins the scientist. "Air and fuel."

You get up out of your chair to check a dial on the wall . . . and crash to the floor!

■ *Turn to page 44.*

"I'd rather have a little more experience at flying this spacecraft before I try to land," you explain. Then you push the master thrust button and pull on the large steering lever. Instantly you're thrown back in your seat as the *Thunderbolt*'s rocket motors roar to life.

"Turn on the forward view screen," says Dr. Granville.

T.O.D. punches a button next to your elbow. You see a huge round blue-gray object floating in the sky ahead of you.

You watch carefully as the dark moon draws closer and closer.

"Look at the size of those craters!" shouts Dr. Granville. "Can't you slow down a little?"

"Not if we're going to get up enough speed to fly up over it," T.O.D. replies.

Callisto fills up the view screen. You're getting so close that you can see small craters, mountains, and valleys. Suddenly one of the mountains blocks your path.

You yank the stick hard and steer around the jagged peak. Ahead of you is clear sky. "We made it!" you shout.

"That's a relief," says Dr. Granville. "While I want to study the moons of

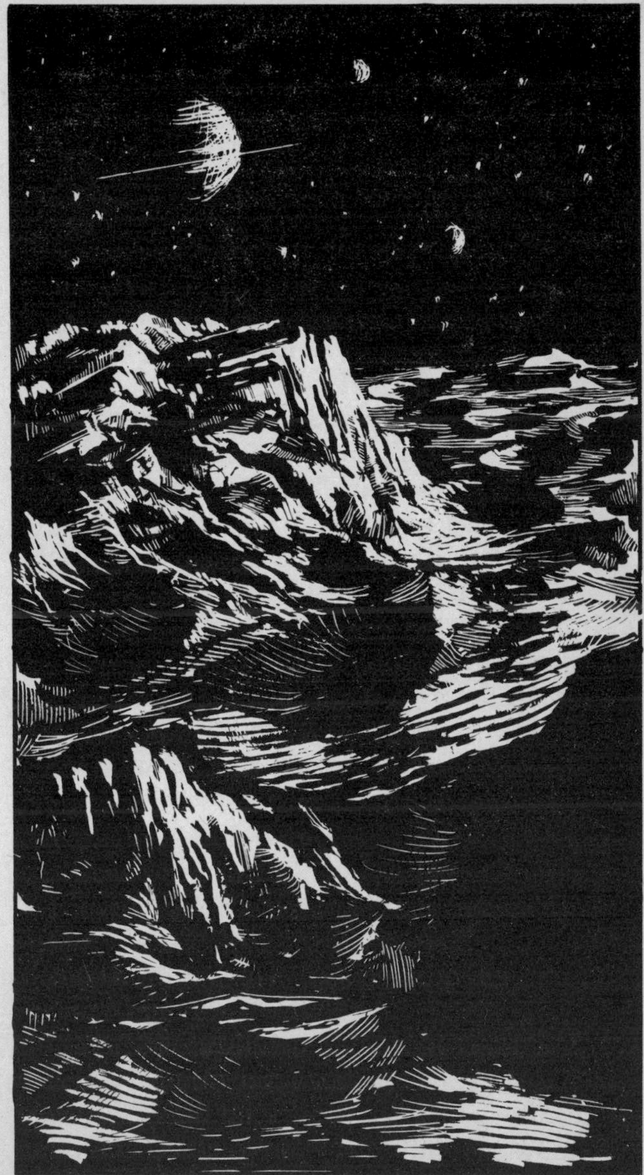

Jupiter, I don't fancy being smashed all over them."

"What's that moon over there?" you ask, pointing to the big shiny orange sphere. Aren't we gaining on it too fast?"

"It's the moon Io," says Dr. Granville. "I think you'd better shut off the rocket engines to save fuel."

You flick off the power switch, but the spacecraft doesn't slow down. "T.O.D., where are the brakes on this jalopy?"

"There aren't any," the android replies. "You have to turn the ship around and apply reverse thrust."

You stare at Jupiter. The huge bright planet fills the view screen. You see thick yellow and orange bands of clouds running around it and a giant red spot swirling in the middle.

"Are those *rings* around Jupiter?" you ask. "I knew the planet Saturn had rings around it, but I didn't know Jupiter did."

"Yes, those are definitely rings," says Dr. Granville. "They're composed of tiny particles. Some scientists think they're the remains of a moon or meteor that broke apart when it flew too close to Jupiter's powerful gravity. The planet Uranus also has rings. However, enough of that. Right now we're moving so fast that we'll enter Jupiter's outer cloud layer in just a few minutes. And we can't let that happen!"

"Why not?"

"Because Jupiter's gravity is so strong that once we get close enough we'll never be able to fly away again. And our ship would be destroyed by the intense heat and pressure of Jupiter's lower atmosphere."

"Wait!" you shout. "There's another moon — dead ahead!"

Dr. Granville squints in the bright light coming from Jupiter. "That must be Amalthea. It's smaller than the other moons we've seen."

"Maybe I can land on it," you suggest.

"That's a possibility," says Dr. Granville. "If we land on Amalthea, we can take off again and head back to one of the bigger moons, where we can search for fuel or air or water."

"We're going so fast that I'm not sure our thruster rockets will slow us down in time," says T.O.D. "We might hit Amalthea too fast to land safely."

"You'd better decide quickly," says Dr. Granville.

■ *Do you want to try to land on Amalthea? Turn to page 56.*

■ *Do you want to keep going and hope you can somehow escape Jupiter's deadly grip? Turn to page 49.*

"Ouch!" you yell, rubbing your knee.

"I bet you'll have a bruise there for a week," says Dr. Granville. He tries not to laugh but can't help himself. "Do you need lessons on how to walk?"

"No," you say, climbing to your feet. "It's just that I haven't been used to gravity in two years."

"Callisto's gravity isn't as strong as Earth's," says T.O.D. "In fact, it's about one fifth as much. If your weight on Earth is seventy-five pounds then you only weigh fifteen pounds on Callisto."

"That's the quickest diet I ever went on," you say. "But let's get back to solving this problem."

You take a step toward the video screen and bounce into the air, crashing your head on the ceiling.

"Yow! This gravity's going to take some getting used to."

Flipping the video screen's camera around, you gaze across the rough surface of Callisto. It looks barren, rocky, and deserted.

"I don't see any gas stations out there," you say, scanning the horizon. "How are we going to find air or fuel?"

"We're probably not going to," the scientist answers. "In fact, I don't think we should even go outside. Callisto is nothing more than a big pile of frozen mud."

Dr. Granville makes a few calculations on his pocket computer. "I think we have to make a choice soon," he says. "Do you think we should search for fuel or air first?"

You think for a moment. "That's a tough choice," you say. "If we get fuel first, we might run out of air and die. If we get air first, we might not have enough fuel to explore for *more* fuel. Which moons are most likely to have fuel or air?"

Dr. Granville is silent for several minutes as he thinks out the answer. Then he speaks. "Ganymede is the most likely to have something we can use for fuel. But for air we'll have to go to Europa *and* Io."

"Why?" you ask.

"Because we need pure water from Europa and Io's heat to transform it into oxygen," the scientist says.

"But if Callisto is made out of mud, isn't there water right in front of us?" you ask.

"Yes," he replies, "but unless the water's very pure, the electrochemical process won't work well. So you've got to decide between going to Europa for water or Ganymede for fuel."

"Air or fuel?" you mutter. "Which is more important?"

You gaze out the window and look at the jagged rock formations of Callisto.

"I'm not sure," you say. "Since we're here, maybe we should explore this moon's surface for a few minutes."

Dr. Granville checks the oxygen meter. "We won't use up any more fuel if we stay here, and we do have enough oxygen to spare for a short trip outside. But I don't recommend it." The scientist sighs. "I will leave the final decision up to you."

"Why don't you let me decide?" asks T.O.D. "I'm perfectly logical."

"If you're so logical, how on earth did you let Mr. Spiro escape? We wouldn't be in this mess if it weren't for you," he answers.

You think about the problem and tell Dr. Granville what you've decided is the best thing to do.

■ *Do you want to explore Callisto's surface now? Turn to page 53.*

■ *Do you want to blast off in search of fuel or air? Turn to page 83.*

Shivers run up and down your spine. "This place gives me the creeps. Something tells me that we should go back."

"But what if the aliens inside are friendly?" asks T.O.D. "After all, they haven't fired at us with any weapons."

"Maybe they want us to walk into a trap," you reply. "We're going back to the *Thunderbolt* immediately."

You gun the engines and turn the crawler around. As you speed away you see a bright flash out of the corner of your eye.

You turn and watch as the alien spaceship shoots up into the air and zooms into space.

"Now we'll never know what was inside," Dr. Granville says. "I wonder if we could have gotten air or fuel from them."

"Maybe I was wrong," you say as the ship flies out of sight into the starry night.

"Well, it certainly would have been interesting to be the first to meet an alien race," exclaims Dr. Granville.

"Unless they wanted to eat us for lunch," you reply, steering a straight course.

48

After a few more minutes, you arrive back at the *Thunderbolt*. You guide the Terra-trak into the elevator hangar and are carried back inside the ship.

Mr. Spiro is still safely locked up. "I knew you wouldn't find anything," he says.

"You wouldn't believe what we saw," Dr. Granville says.

"That's right," you agree. "Nobody would ever believe us — good thing you took pictures."

■ *You, Dr. Granville, and T.O.D. go up to the control room. Turn to page 83.*

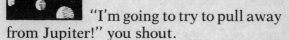

"I'm going to try to pull away from Jupiter!" you shout.

"It's too late, it's too late," says Dr. Granville. "We'll never make it."

"I wouldn't say that," offers T.O.D. "We have a one percent chance of avoiding Jupiter's gravity if our angle of movement is just right."

You push on the thruster button until your thumb turns white as all the blood drains out of it. The *Thunderbolt* vibrates so much that you feel as if your eyes are going to rattle right out of your skull.

The planet Jupiter fills the whole video screen in front of you. You can see the cloud layers moving across the surface and the Great Red Spot violently whirling around.

"Amazing," says Dr. Granville. "We're able to see the rings of Jupiter up close. I can actually see the tiny particles that make up the rings."

You don't even glance up as you use all your strength to try to coax more speed out of the rocket motors.

50

Suddenly everything becomes quiet — very quiet. The motors have stopped. You check the gauge, but you already know the answer: There's not a drop of fuel left.

The cabin begins to heat up.

"That's the radiation from Jupiter," explains Dr. Granville.

"No one on Earth will know what really happened," you tell him. "I guess Mr. Spiro will get his revenge after all."

"And I guess winning a lottery isn't always lucky," says Dr. Granville. "I'm happy to see Jupiter up this close even if it's only for a few more minutes. Just look at those frightfully fabulous cloud formations!"

"I knew there were risks when I bought my ticket," you answer bravely.

"What about me?" asks T.O.D. "Nobody even asked me if I wanted to come along. I could have been a robot gardener somewhere nice and safe."

"Look!" you exclaim. "The sky of Jupiter is bright blue. It's almost like Earth's sky."

"Except," adds Dr. Granville, "that it's made up of hydrogen, helium, and ammonia."

"I can feel Jupiter's gravity pulling us down," you say, "The clouds are glowing orange, red, yellow, and brown. I've never seen anything like it."

WHAM!

"What was that?" you shout. The screen lights up for a second and then goes dark.

WHAM!

"Something's tossing us around! Did we hit something?"

"That's impossible," replies Dr. Granville. "Jupiter's just a bunch of clouds that get more and more condensed as we go deeper. But we're not deep enough to have hit the liquid layer yet!"

WHAM!

Suddenly the inside of the cabin is ablaze in a blinding display of light. Sparks shoot out of the control panel. You turn and see T.O.D. glowing like a Fourth of July sparkler.

"Dr. Granville! What's going on?" you shout.

"Lightning!" he answers. "The thunderbolts of Jupiter. Jupiter was the ancient god of the Romans. When he was mad at somebody, he'd throw a thunderbolt at them. I guess old Jupiter — "

WHAM!

" — doesn't like visitors!"

"That's just a legend," you reply.

"Perhaps," answers Dr. Granville, "but the charges in Jupiter's clouds build up just like the clouds on Earth. We're being struck by Jupiter-sized lightning!"

WHAM!

You're knocked out of your seat and thrown on the floor. Your head hits the control panel and you are knocked unconscious.

The whole cabin is on fire with electricity.

WHAM!

Lightning strikes again and again. The spacecraft is engulfed in flames.

THE END

"I think we should briefly explore Callisto first," you say. "We may stumble on something valuable. If we don't take too much time, we won't use a lot of our remaining air."

"I won't use any," says T.O.D.

"That's a big help," Dr. Granville says. "Let's get the Terra-trak Crawler on the road."

"I didn't see any roads on the video screen," says T.O.D.

"It's an old expression," the scientist explains. "Here, slip this on." He hands you a pressurized helmet with a viewvisor. "Just activate the hear-speak switch."

"What's the Terra-trak Crawler?" you ask, locking the helmet into place and switching on the hear-speak switch.

"A small vehicle designed to explore any surface," explains T.O.D. "It will protect you from radiation, cold, and lack of oxygen."

"Sounds like I shouldn't leave home without it."

The android leads the way down to the

storage compartments, two decks below.

"Did we land on something?" George Spiro yells from his cell over the intercom network as you enter.

"We're on Callisto," answers Dr. Granville. "No thanks to you."

"I'm sure you'll find nothing here but rocks," the pilot screams. "I hope you all die!"

"We'll do our best to disappoint you," Dr. Granville says. "Come on, let's see what secrets we can find."

T.O.D. opens a hatch and the three of you crawl through it, leaving Mr. Spiro behind.

Inside a tiny room you see a vehicle the size of a small subcompact car. It has two treaded balloon wheels on each side and a thick glass shield on top.

You climb in. It's a tight squeeze, but you manage. Dr. Granville pushes a button.

WHIRRR!

The vehicle is gently lowered and you realize you're in a small elevator.

"Next floor, home furnishings, luggage, and the moon Callisto," jokes Dr. Granville.

■ *Turn to page 58.*

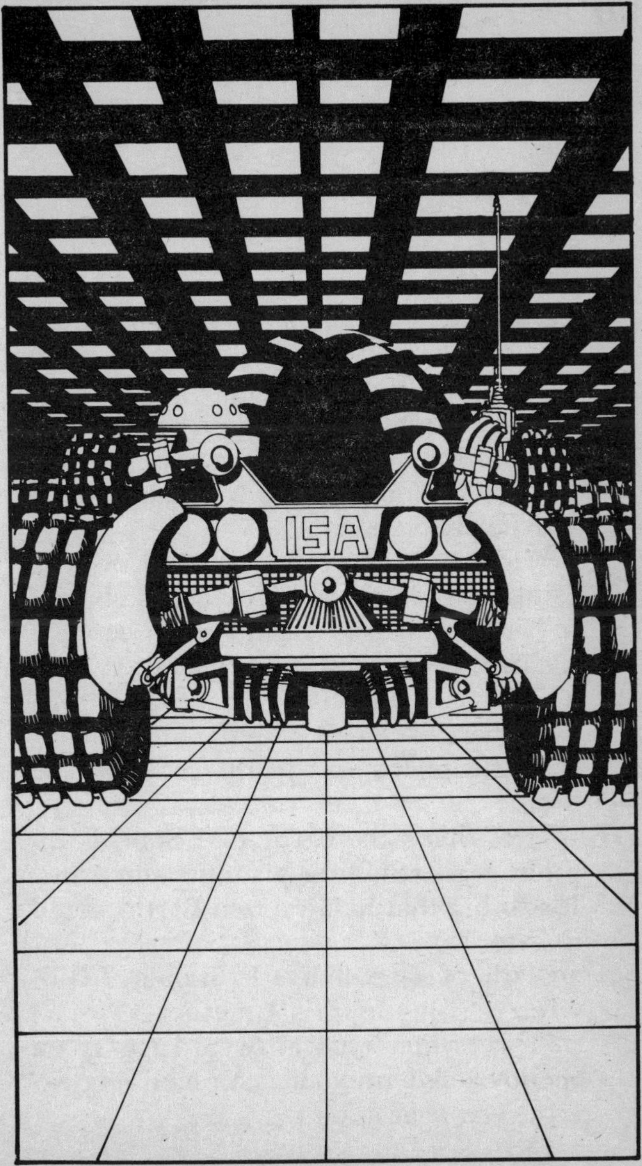
ISA

"I'm going to try to land on Amalthea!" you shout. "Hang on."

You quickly stab the main thruster button and are thrown back into your seat as the *Thunderbolt* thrusts forward.

CLANG! You hear T.O.D. crash into the bulkhead behind you.

"Hold on!" you yell over the deafening sound of the engine. "Why is it so bright in here?" you ask. "I can barely see."

"The sun's reflecting off Jupiter," explains Dr. Granville. "That's Amalthea over there."

"I thought it was in the center!" you shout.

"No, that's the Great Red Spot of Jupiter. It's actually a gigantic hurricane. It's so big that half a dozen Earths could fit into it."

"Pull over, pull over!" shouts T.O.D. "You're going to miss Amalthea."

"I'm trying," you answer. Tugging on the joystick with your last remaining energy, you hear a loud . . .

CRACK!

"It broke off! The stick broke!" you shout.

Furiously you grab the remaining stubby part of the joystick and yank at the broken metal.

"More speed!" shouts Dr. Granville. "We're drifting away from Amalthea."

"I'm trying, I'm trying!" you scream. One hand is on the thruster button and the other's trying to keep the broken joystick pointed in the right direction.

"My sensors indicate that it is growing warmer in here," says T.O.D.

"That's the radiation," explains Dr. Granville.

"Here comes Amalthea!" you yell. "I think we can make it after all."

The tiny white moon rushes toward you.

And just as suddenly is gone.

"There goes Amalthea," Dr. Granville says.

"I hope it's not the last anyone will ever see of us," you solemnly reply. "I wonder which of the theories about Jupiter is correct?"

"Which ones?" says Dr. Granville.

"About whether we'll be crushed or melted first."

■ *For a trip down to Jupiter, turn to page 49.*

KA-THUNK.

The elevator stops.

Dr. Granville pushes another button. A large door opens onto Callisto. Through the Terra-trak bubble shield you see the dark brown rocky surface of a deep crater ahead of you. In the sky you see stars — millions of stars.

"They look odd," you say.

"That's because they're not twinkling," explains the scientist. "There's no air on Callisto, so you're seeing the stars as they really are."

"This is great!" you say. Giant craters are all around you. Straight ahead you can see Jupiter. Horizontal bands of orange, red, and brown clouds cross its glowing surface. "It looks HUGE!"

"It is," says Dr. Granville. "A thousand Earths could fit inside it."

"Let's get going," you shout eagerly. "I want to see what's on this moon."

He shows you the controls. You push the accelerator with your foot and grab the steering wheel tightly.

ZOOM!

The Terra-trak speeds forward and races up the side of the crater.

"Hey, this is fun!" you shout.

You drive down into another crater. And another. They all look alike. Some are bigger than others, but you realize that craters are just holes in the ground.

Suddenly you spot something up ahead.

"What's that?" asks Dr. Granville.

"It looks like it's metal," says T.O.D. "It's smooth and shiny."

"Maybe it's a hamburger stand!" you say. "I knew it was a good idea to explore Callisto."

You speed toward the huge object.

"It's some kind of spaceship," you say.

The gigantic metal ship is bigger than an aircraft carrier. The gray metal surface has long spikes covering every inch of it. Columns of red dots run up and down the sides.

"Maybe there's someone or something inside, and they can give us a ride home."

"Let's hope they're friendly blokes," says Dr. Granville. "It would be very exciting to be the first human to greet an alien being."

"Perhaps they'll have androids inside," speculates T.O.D. "Then I'd have somebody who'd appreciate me."

"Oh, we appreciate you," you say with a chuckle.

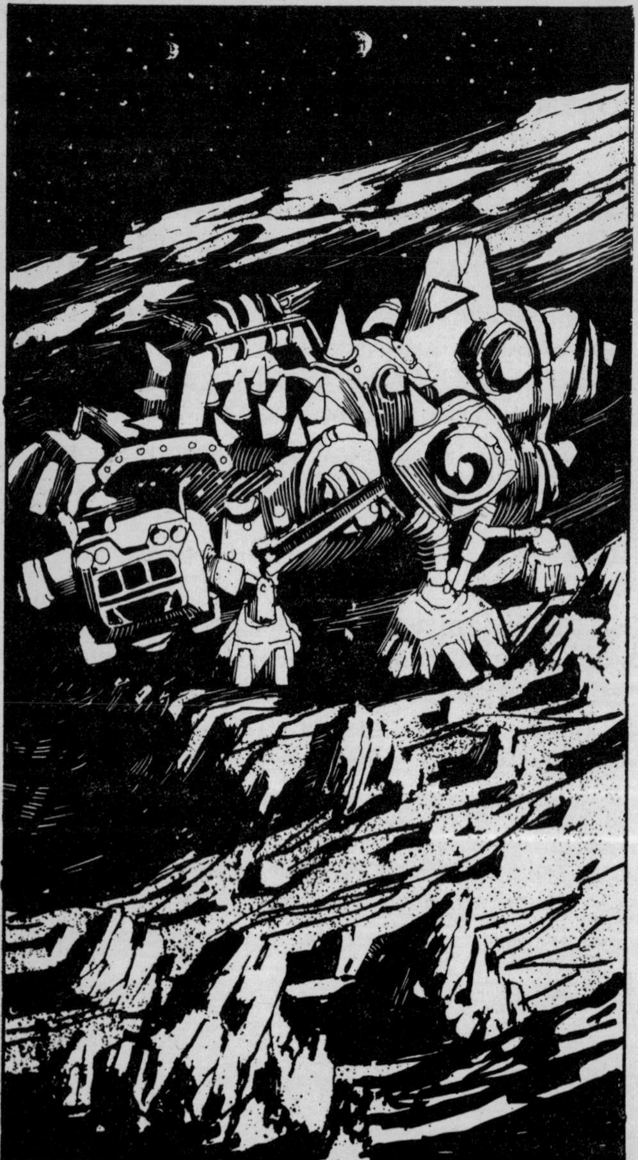

You drive closer to the huge alien spacecraft. It's as big as a battleship. "I wonder what we should do," you say. "Do we go up to the front door and knock? Or sneak around back? I don't see any lights."

Dr. Granville is busy taking pictures. "We shouldn't get out of the Terra-trak," he says. "Who knows what's inside that spacecraft?"

"I could go inside and look," volunteers T.O.D.

"Let's get out of here," says Dr. Granville. "We can always return to Callisto after we replenish our air and fuel." He turns to you. "What do you think we should do?"

■ *Do you want to let T.O.D. explore the alien spaceship? Turn to page 69.*

■ *Do you want to go back to your own ship now? Turn to page 47.*

You see the readout on the tiny screen:

MOLECULE COMPOSITION:
2 PARTS OXYGEN
1 PART NITROGEN
1 PART CARBON
3 PARTS HYDROGEN

Dr. Granville tries to scratch his head. But his space helmet stops his gloved hand. You laugh.

"What does the readout mean?" you ask. "Can we burn it?"

"I'm not sure," says the scientist. "The combination is familiar, but I can't quite remember what it is."

"I think it's known as nitromethane," says T.O.D. "I read a data tape on organic chemistry last week."

"Nitromethane!" says Dr. Granville. "It was right on the tip of my tongue."

"Does it taste good?" T.O.D. asks. "I thought nitromethane was poisonous to humans."

"It is," the scientist replies. "But rocket scientists love to eat it for breakfast!"

Dr. Granville smiles at you and shakes

his head. "Nitromethane is a bit unstable, but we can certainly use it for rocket fuel."

"Great!" you cheer.

Using the front of the crawler as a scoop, you push a big mound of the frozen fuel toward the *Thunderbolt*.

You go inside the ship and send T.O.D. back outside to shovel the orange chemical into the rocket tanks.

As you and Dr. Granville make sure that the Terra-trak was not damaged when you plowed into the frozen nitromethane, George Spiro screams, "You'll never escape from this moon alive!"

"Don't count your alligators before they're hatched," replies Dr. Granville. "We've just found some excellent rocket fuel on Ganymede. In fact, there's enough fuel out there to power hundreds of space colonies for a long, long time."

"But you'll still run out of air," cackles the pilot.

"Not necessarily," the scientist answers. "We're going to get water on Europa and change it to oxygen on Io."

"That's impossible," Spiro snaps. "You'll never do it."

"Yes we will," you yell defiantly.

"That's the spirit," Dr. Granville says. "Come on, let's blast off."

Moments later, T.O.D. comes back inside the spaceship. "You're fueled up and ready to go," he informs you. The three of you quickly climb up to the control room.

"Set the course for Europa," Dr. Granville says.

"Which one?" T.O.D. asks. "Should we go the long way around Jupiter or should we take a shortcut?"

"Shortcut?"

"Yes," the android explains. "If we go close enough to Jupiter, we can get there in a few hours. Otherwise it will take us a day to catch up with Europa's orbit."

You think for a moment.

"But won't it be more dangerous," you ask, "if we go close to Jupiter?"

"Yes," answers T.O.D. "But our air supply — or should I say — *your* air supply is running low."

You quickly make up your mind.

■ *Do you want to take the safe but longer way to get to Europa? Turn to page 84.*

■ *Do you want to take the shortcut to Europa? Turn to page 93.*

You cross your fingers for good luck. With the rockets blasting beneath you, you come in for a landing.

You glance at the video screen.

"I see stars!" you shout.

"What were you expecting to see?" asks T.O.D. "Eggplants?"

"No," you explain cheerfully. "I was afraid we'd burst through the ice."

"My calculations indicated that it would be thick enough to hold us," says Dr. Granville.

"All right!" you cheer. "Let's get our water and head for Io."

You, Dr. Granville, and T.O.D. put on space suits. "These seem so bulky," you say.

"That's because they have tiny wires inside that create an electric field around our bodies," the scientist explains. "If we didn't have it, we'd be fried by the intense particles of deadly radiation coming from Jupiter."

You and Dr. Granville go outside and begin exploring. You leap and slide across the pure ice surface of Europa, lighter on your feet than you would be at home. "This is better than an ice rink," you shout into your suit's microphone.

"And without any stupid organ music," agrees the scientist. "On Europa you only weigh half of what you did on Callisto, so your muscles can let you jump even higher."

Jupiter looms overhead. You spot several other moons in the sky.

"What's that star?" you ask. "It seems really bright."

"It's the Sun," explains Dr. Granville. "We're so far away from it that it's only a little bit brighter than a normal star."

"Where should we dig for water?"

"Anywhere," says Dr. Granville, unpacking a portable expansion drill from his toolpack. Seconds later the drill is boring into the thick glistening ice.

Suddenly you feel a rumble beneath your feet. You jump back.

A gusher of water shoots out of the ice.

"We struck water!" you shout.

"What's that?" asks T.O.D.

"You mean you don't know what water is?" you ask. "I thought you were programmed with all kinds of knowledge."

"I am," replies the android. "But I was not referring to water. That's made up of hydrogen and oxygen. I was referring to

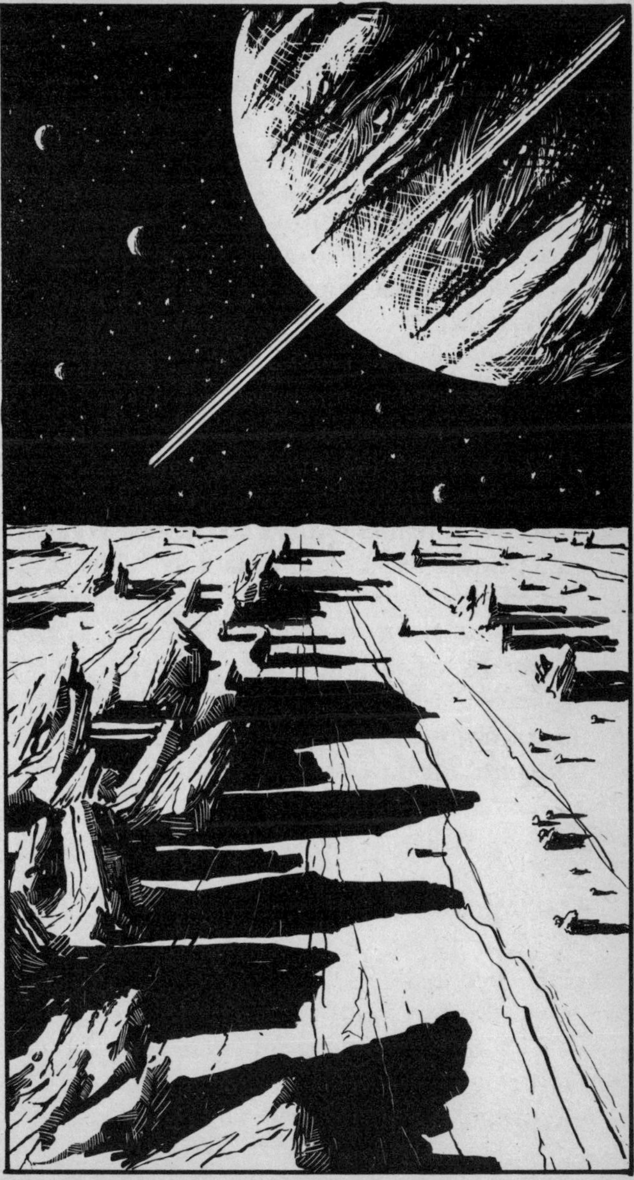

those aliens who have just surrounded us."

"Aliens!" you shout, looking up. A dozen blue globe-shaped vehicles are floating in the air around you.

One of the ships dives down and zooms over your head. A green ray shoots out.

WHOMP!

A hole appears in the ice in front of you. Water gushes out and you jump back.

"What should we do?" asks T.O.D.

"We can try to take off and outrun them," says Dr. Granville, looking at you. "Or we can meet them in peace. You're the pilot, so you should decide."

■ *Do you want to escape the aliens? Turn to page 71.*

■ *Do you want to try to communicate with them? Turn to page 74.*

You pull the Terra-trak up beside what looks like an entrance hatch. "T.O.D., I think it would be safest if you go inside first."

"All right," says the android. "But if they blast me, I won't like it."

"Don't be silly," you reply. "If they wanted to blast us, they would have done so right away."

T.O.D. climbs through the small air lock in the side of the Terra-trak. He wiggles out onto the surface and bounces up to the hatch of the alien spaceship. His body moves easily in the low gravity. You watch as he presses a small button on the side.

The hatch opens!

The inside is dark, but T.O.D. switches on the atomic floodlight in one of his arms and steps inside. The hatch snaps shut.

"I hope we didn't make a mistake," you say. "Maybe we should go back."

"Let's wait for fifteen minutes," says Dr. Granville.

You sit inside the Terra-trak Crawler and wait.

Just as you're about to retreat, the hatch opens again.

"It's T.O.D.!" you say. The android crawls into the Terra-trak through the air lock.

"You made it!" you cheer.

"I have something to tell you," says T.O.D.

"What did the aliens say?" you ask. "Will they help us? Were you able to make them understand? What do they look like?"

"The aliens are robots."

"But can they help us?" you continue.

"They could, but they won't," replies the android. "They convinced me that humans aren't as good as robots."

"What!" you shout in amazement. "I don't understand."

"Of course you don't . . . human!" T.O.D. reaches for your throat with two of his arms.

Dr. Granville tries to pull him loose. But the android has two more arms. He strangles the scientist quickly.

"Since you were nicer to me," it says, "I'll let you live longer."

"How much longer?"

"One second."

His steel fingers tighten around your throat. Tighter and tighter until. . . .

THE END

"Let's get the heck out of here!" you shout, racing toward your spaceship.

You make it safely back without the aliens blasting you to bits.

"Maybe they're not really hostile," suggests T.O.D. as you climb back inside the *Thunderbolt*. "They could have just been looking for water like us. I wonder what kind of beings they were?"

"Maybe," you reply, "they're deadly blobs of Jell-O who want to eat *us* for dessert. I don't want to find out!"

Dr. Granville laughs, and you climb into the pilot's chair and hit the rocket motors. The *Thunderbolt* leaps into the sky. You steer right past the strange blue alien ships, but they don't follow.

"Whew," you say when you're out of sight. "That was close."

"Head for Io," says Dr. Granville. "We have enough water to manufacture oxygen now."

"You bet!" you reply. T.O.D. shows you how to set the computer for Io, which is on the other side of Jupiter.

"How long will it take us to get there?" you ask the android.

"About forty years," it answers.

"I think you miscalculated," Dr. Granville says. "I always knew that you had a bad chip in you."

"My calculations are correct," T.O.D. insists. "It will take forty years because we will run out of fuel."

"But why?" you ask. "I thought we had enough fuel."

Dr. Granville investigates the fuel meter. "No, that renegade rust-bucket is right. We used up too much fuel in the last takeoff."

You sigh. "I should have gone to Ganymede first," you say.

Suddenly the rocket motors are silent.

"That's the last of our fuel," says T.O.D.

"And the last of us," Dr. Granville adds. "We'll orbit Jupiter until our air runs out."

"That's not correct," the android explains. "We'll orbit Jupiter for thousands of years."

Dr. Granville reaches over and hits a small switch on T.O.D.'s chest.

"What did you do?" you ask.

"I shut it off," explains the scientist. "I'd like my last few hours to be spent without listening to that robot's mindless chatter. Would you like to play cards?"

Having nothing better to do, you and Dr. Granville play poker.

You win!

But you won't be able to spend the money.

THE END

You raise your arms in peace. "We're friends," you shout into your suit's radio transmitter.

But the aliens don't seem to understand your language. They fly around for a few more minutes. Then they land! Strange aliens roll out of the ships. They look like blobs of grape Jell-O with olives for eyes and carrots for arms and legs.

Before you can flee, the aliens surround you. They don't seem hostile, but they won't let you return to the *Thunderbolt*.

The aliens explore your ship and return with Mr. Spiro, tied up with ropes. The four of you are herded into one of the alien ships. It's so bright inside that you can't see a thing. Suddenly they take off and fly you out of the solar system.

Finally you arrive at what looks like a gigantic floating space platform. The aliens take you out and present you to a three-headed woman who speaks English.

"Where are we?" you ask.

"This is the Interplanetary Zoo," she answers. "You'll be quite comfortable here."

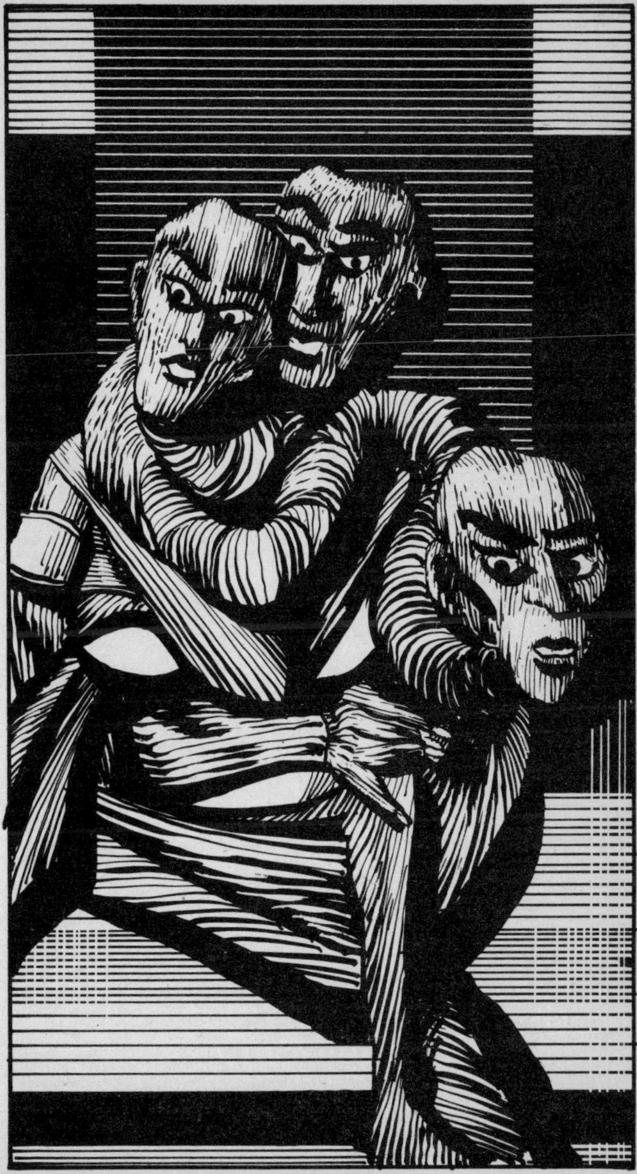

"But I want to go home!"

"You can't," replies one head.

"The zoo needs more humans," another says.

"Let me show you to your cage," the third says.

THE END

"Let's head for Ganymede," you say. "Once we have enough fuel, we can reach the other moons more easily."

"Your logic is good," T.O.D. says. "That is what I would have said."

You swiftly guide the *Thunderbolt* through space. A few hours pass when all of a sudden you spot the lumpy surface of Ganymede looming up on the video screen. "Hang on," you shout. "We're going to land."

"I just hope we don't run out of fuel before we land," T.O.D. replies.

"Me, too," you say. "The gauge is right on empty."

You fire the steering rockets. The *Thunderbolt* spins around until its main thruster rockets are facing toward Ganymede.

"Don't use up too much fuel," cautions Dr. Granville. "We've got to be careful."

"There isn't much choice," you say, keeping a close eye on your speed indicator. "If we don't find fuel here, we'll never have enough to fly to any of the other moons."

"I guess it's a good thing that I don't

have any feelings," T.O.D. says. "Otherwise I'd be very frightened."

The northern ice cap of Ganymede now fills up your video screen. "I guess one patch of snow is as good as another," you say. "Hang on, we're going down!"

You count off the feet . . . 5,000 . . . 4,000 . . . 3,000 . . . 1,000 . . . WHUMP!

"We made it!" you shout, switching off the rocket motor. "And we've even got a little bit of fuel left."

"How much?" asks T.O.D.

"About enough to boil a good strong cup of tea!" Dr. Granville replies. "But I'm certain we'll find chemicals that we can use for fuel."

You examine the terrain on the video screen. "It looks like the dead of winter out there," you say. "But I've never seen snowbanks like that! Blue, green, yellow, and silver."

"That's because the snow here isn't made up of just water. Most of it is methane or ammonia."

"It sure looks unusual," you say. "Big patches of different colors. How come it's not all mixed together?"

"I'm not sure, but I suspect it's because there's no rain, wind, or erosion on Ganymede. Whatever was put there in the first place is still there."

"Let's go see it," you say. "Are you ready to explore Ganymede?"

"Quite ready," says Dr. Granville. "You and that noisy robot meet me at the Terra-trak Crawler in the lowest compartment."

You and the android climb down to the bottom of the *Thunderbolt* and wait for Dr. Granville.

"It's a good thing George Spiro didn't wreck the crawler, too," you say. "We'd never be able to find anything without it."

"The Terra-trak won't help you," shouts the pilot from inside his locked storage cabin. "You'll never find anything on Ganymede except methane and ammonia! And you can't use them for fuel."

"Not according to my theories, old boy," says Dr. Granville as he joins you. "While it's true that Earth spectroscopes have picked up large amounts of methane and ammonia, I believe that other organic compounds can exist that are mixtures of methane's and ammonia's atoms: carbon, oxygen, nitrogen, and hydrogen. And one of those mixtures might make a dandy rocket fuel."

"But how will we find it?" you ask.

"That's where the portable atomic analyzer comes in," he says, patting a small box under his arm.

"You'll fail!" shouts Mr. Spiro.

"No way!" you reply confidently.

Dr. Granville nearly bumps into T.O.D. as he steps around to the Terra-trak Crawler. "I'd very much appreciate it if you'd be so kind as to get out of my way," grumbles Dr. Granville. "We haven't got all day."

"That's right," agrees T.O.D. "A day on Ganymede is only one hundred and seventy-two hours."

You climb inside the small vehicle. T.O.D. and Dr. Granville, with the atomic analyzer on his knees, squeeze in beside you.

"Ganymede, here we come!" you say.

Dr. Granville presses the elevator remote control button.

With a loud humming noise, the Terra-trak Crawler is lowered to the surface of the moon.

"It's brighter out here than on Callisto," you say, shielding your eyes.

"That's because we're closer to Jupiter," explains Dr. Granville.

"Where's the Sun?" you ask.

"We can't see it from here," the scientist answers. "But it's not much brighter than a star in Earth's sky at night. Most of the light we'll see here will be reflected from Jupiter."

"Jupiter sure is bright," you say.

"It's like a gigantic mirror," Dr. Gran-

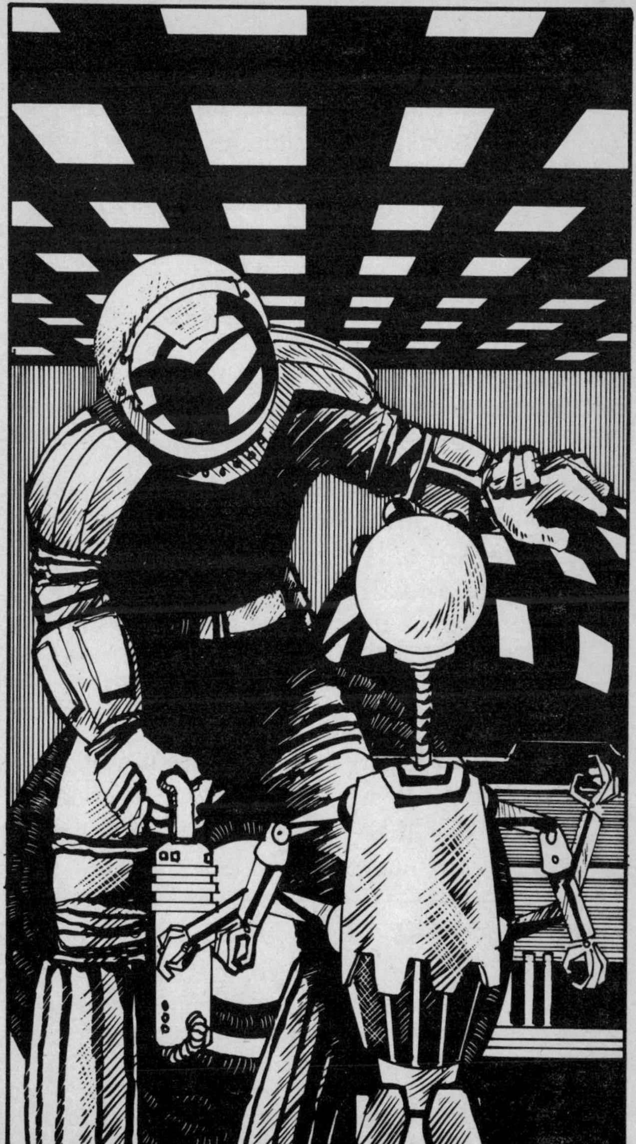

ville explains. "Also, since we're in the middle of the north polar ice cap of Ganymede, the ices here reflect even more light to our eyes."

"Where do we start?" you ask, driving the crawler over a blue-colored snowbank.

"One patch is as good as another," Dr. Granville replies. "Try that orange one over there."

The Terra-trak's treads bite into the snow and carry you forward.

Suddenly you slip back! You jam on the brakes. "Hang on tight," you shout. Then you gun the engine even harder. The crawler's treads bite into the snow.

You slip again. But this time you race the engine as hard as you can and climb over the hill.

ZOOM!

You shoot down the other side.

You pull up to the orange patch of ice. Dr. Granville activates the atomic analyzer. "We'll have a reading in seconds."

You wait nervously.

■ *To see what you've found, turn to page 62.*

"I think we should take off right now," you say.

"Before we do," warns Dr. Granville, "push that pink button over there."

"Okay," you reply, pressing it. "What does it do?"

"It sends out a remote-controlled robot arm that scoops up samples from the ground below us. That way, if we ever get back to Earth, scientists can determine what elements are present on each of the moons we land on."

"But which moon are you going to go to next?" asks T.O.D. "You've got so many to choose from."

"Not really," Dr. Granville explains. "We need air and fuel. To find air we should go to Europa and then to Io. But our best bet for finding fuel is Ganymede."

You think hard. Which is more important? Air or fuel? Finally you decide.

■ *Do you want to go to Europa and begin your search for air? Turn to page 95.*

■ *Do you want to blast off for Ganymede and look for more fuel? Turn to page 77.*

"I think I'll take the safe orbit," you say.

As soon as T.O.D. calculates your course, you blast off and leave Ganymede behind.

T.O.D. goes below to feed George Spiro while you and Dr. Granville finally eat dinner.

"I don't know if I can get used to having to eat all my food by sucking through a straw," you say.

"But that's the only way we can be sure it won't make a mess all over the walls," Dr. Granville explains. "Ordinary food would float away when we don't have gravity."

"Even so, I sure would like a nice bowl of soup."

"It would turn into little floating blobs of soup," says the scientist. "But maybe that would be more fun. We could play Ping-Pong with our breakfast, basketball with our lunch, and pool with our dinner."

"No thanks," you mutter. "I gave up playing with my food when I was two!"

Time passes slowly, and you begin to feel sleepy. You yawn. Dr. Granville yawns.

Suddenly he jumps out of his chair and floats over to a panel on the wall.

"Great jumping jackrabbits!" he shouts. "We're running out of air. That's why we've been yawning so much."

"Oh, no," you moan. "I shouldn't have taken the long way to Europa. Now we're doomed."

T.O.D. climbs up the ladder. "What's wrong?" he says. "You two look gloomy. Why aren't you happy? We found nitromethane, didn't we?"

"Yes," you explain. "But we're running out of air."

"Why don't you get back into the Sonarest chambers?" suggests the android. "Then you can sleep, and I'll prepare the fuel to fly you home."

You think a moment. You don't like the idea of failing on your mission to explore the rest of the moons of Jupiter, but you don't like the idea of dying either.

"All right," you decide. "We'll allow ourselves to be frozen and you take us home."

"And don't get lost!" grumbles Dr. Granville.

The three of you go down and safely tie up George Spiro. After you put him in his Sonarest chamber, you and Dr. Granville climb into yours.

You're frozen again. You sleep. You dream. Time passes. . . .

One day, in the middle of a nice dream about skiing on Ganymede, you wake up.

T.O.D.'s face greets you. He opens the green door.

"Are we there yet?" you ask.

"We're back at Earth," explains the android. "But you might not like it."

"Why not?" you ask. "I can't wait to see it again."

"Things have changed," T.O.D. says.

"How much can change in two years?"

"It isn't two years," T.O.D. explains. "I miscalculated the direction and went the long way home. A thousand years have gone by."

"Wait a minute!" you shout. "You're joking."

The android shakes his round metal head. "No, I'm not joking. I managed to repair the radio. Listen to what I'm picking up."

You hear a babble of voices coming from the speaker.

You wake up Dr. Granville and explain.

"I knew that rust-eating robot couldn't be trusted," the scientist grumbles.

"At least we're home," you say.

But after you land on Earth, you're not sure it's home anymore. A thousand years have changed everything. People now paint their bodies green, walk on their hands everywhere, and you can't seem to figure out any of the million languages that everyone speaks. And the worst part of it is that people think *you* are really strange. They laugh and point at you everywhere you go.

THE END

"All right, let's go rescue the android," you say. "But how are we going to do it? If we go too close to Jupiter we'll be pulled into its gravity."

"There's a way we might be able to," says Dr. Granville. "If we calculate everything precisely, we might be able to do what's called a slingshot."

"What's that?"

"We can use Jupiter's gravity to actually speed us up so much that we swing *around* the planet instead of crashing into it. But we have to fly the spacecraft at just the right angle."

"You're the math whiz," you tell him. "If you can program the course computer, I'll steer the ship."

"I can attempt it," he answers.

You try to call T.O.D. on the radio, but he's out of range.

Finally Dr. Granville is finished with his calculations. "That ought to do it," he says.

You turn the *Thunderbolt* around and speed after T.O.D. When you're in range, you call out to him on the short-range radio.

"Thunderbolt to T.O.D. Can you hear me?"

"Certainly," replies the android. "You don't have to shout."

"We're coming to pick you up."

"Thank you," it says. "But be sure to take a look at Jupiter. The view is spectacular."

As you race toward the android, you and Dr. Granville examine the planet more closely.

"Look at the rings," the scientist says. "While not as big as Saturn's, they are still quite beautiful."

But nothing looks as inspiring as the planet Jupiter below you. Bands of orange-colored gases swirl across the giant planet's face and the Great Red Spot in the middle looks like a giant eye. "Some scientists think it is colored red by sulfur dust from Io's volcanoes," says Dr. Granville.

"Don't get too caught up in the view," says T.O.D. "You're getting close to me."

"That rascal robot is sure a pain in the neck," says Dr. Granville. "Maybe we shouldn't . . . oh, all right, I give up. Let's haul him in."

While you steer, Dr. Granville puts on his space suit and goes into the air lock. He throws a jet-propelled rope to T.O.D., reels him in, and closes the outer air lock.

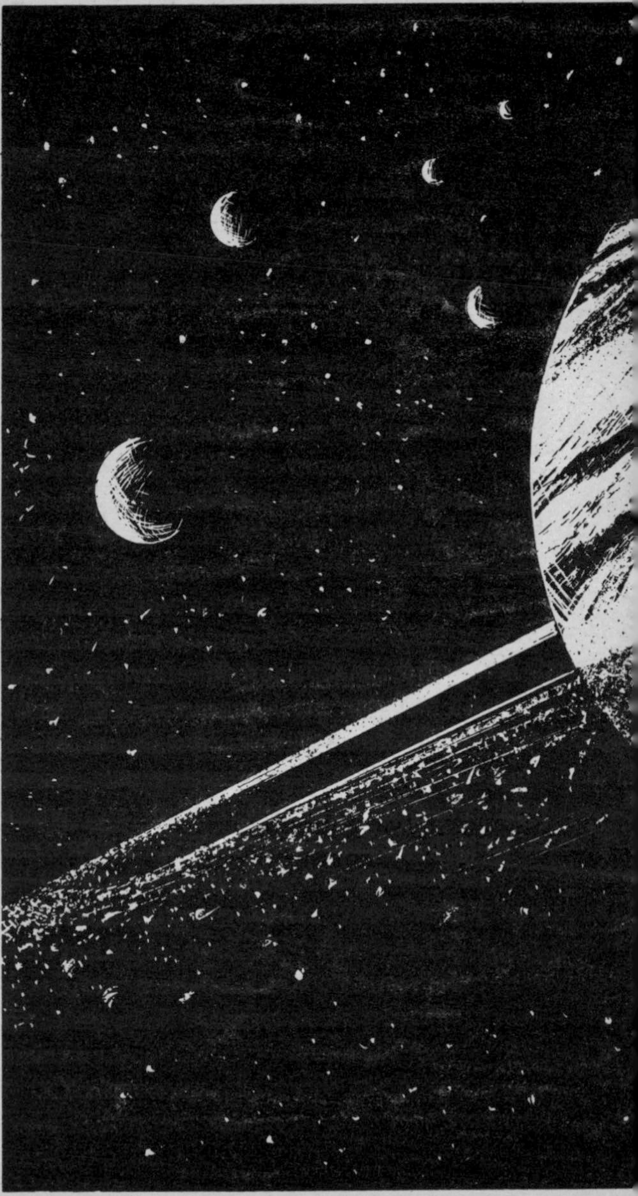

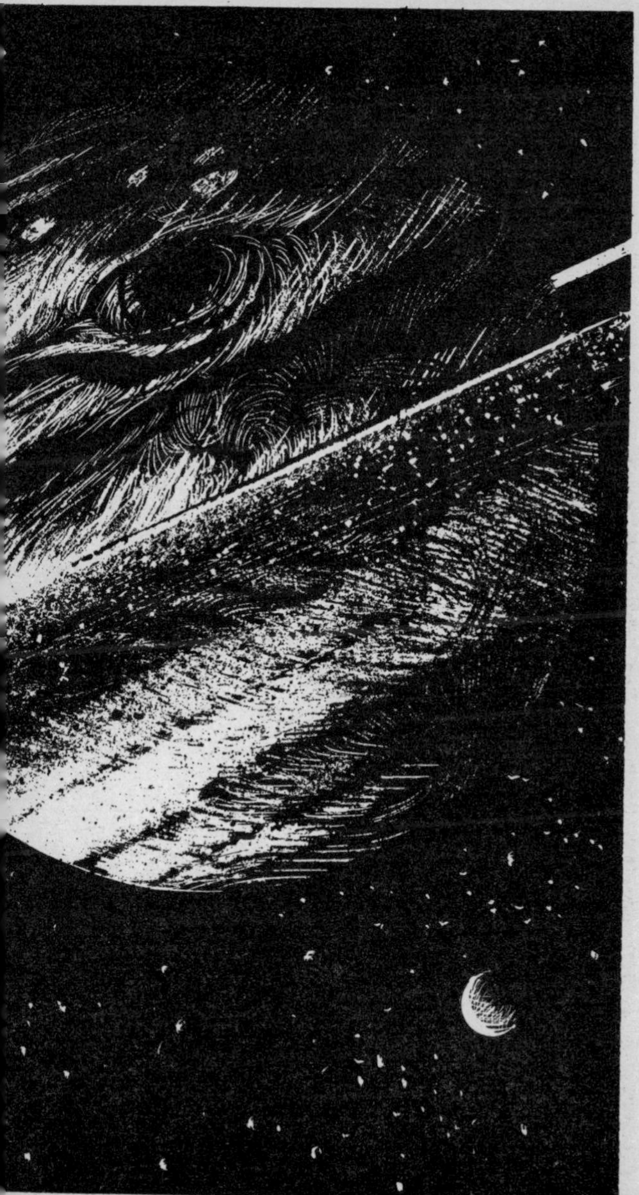

"Hi," says the android when he pops through the inner air-lock door. "Any mail for me while I was gone?"

You groan. "Same old robot," you say, turning to greet him.

"Ugh," adds Dr. Granville. "What a horrible sense of humor. Let's get into those Sonarest chambers so we can sleep the rest of the way home and not have to hear any more from T.O.D."

"All right with me," replies the android. "I like it when it's nice and quiet."

T.O.D. brings George Spiro up and puts him in a Sonarest chamber. When he hears that the mission was a success, he just scowls and doesn't say a word.

"I'll be the pilot," offers T.O.D. "We'll get home safe and sound."

Then you and Dr. Granville climb into your chambers and are soon in a deep and chilly sleep.

■ *When you're through sleeping, turn to page 111.*

"We'd better not risk running out of oxygen," you say. "Chart a course as close to Jupiter as you can, T.O.D."

"But not too close!" cautions Dr. Granville.

In a matter of seconds the android tells you which direction to go. You blast off and head for Europa.

But as you fly through space, you see Jupiter looming larger and larger on the video screen.

"I don't know about this," you say sadly. "Maybe I made a mistake."

"It's too late now," Dr. Granville says. "If you try to change our course now, we'll crash into Jupiter for sure."

Crossing your fingers for good luck, you hang on and hope.

You wait . . . and wait!

You spot a shiny blue-white moon ahead of you!

"Europa!" shouts Dr. Granville. "We made it. Land quickly."

Using your new-found skill as a rocket pilot, you quickly set down on the smooth surface of Europa.

"It's solid ice," you say.

"That's right," Dr. Granville says. "It's a big ocean of water coated by a thick layer of ice."

Moving as fast as you can, the three of you go out onto the surface and drill a hole in the ice. You wear special space suits that protect you from the radiation that Jupiter gives off. Water spurts up and you pipe it into the empty tanks of the *Thunderbolt*.

"There's enough water to supply the needs of thousands of space colonies here on Europa," you say as you climb back into the control cabin. "And it looks purer than any water I ever saw on Earth!"

"That's right," Dr. Granville agrees. "And we've proved that there's rocket fuel on Ganymede. According to my calculations, there are enough energy-producing materials on that moon to keep Earth running for centuries."

"But," T.O.D. reminds you, "if you don't change that water into air soon, nobody will know *what* you've found, because we won't live to tell about it."

"Brrr," you shiver. "Let's get going."

"Head for Io," says Dr. Granville. "And make it snappy! The future of the human race is depending on YOU!"

■ *Blast off for Io and turn to page 102.*

"I think Europa is where we should go first," you say. Then you initiate takeoff, and the *Thunderbolt* leaps into the star-filled sky.

When you're safely away from Callisto, you ask Dr. Granville to explain more about how he hopes to replenish your air supply by going to Europa.

"Certainly," he answers.

"I wonder if he can explain it in less than ten thousand words," says T.O.D. "I've noticed that Dr. Granville talks on and on and on."

"That's because I have something original to say," the scientist replies with a grin. "*You* are just a high-priced tape recorder."

Dr. Granville turns to you. "My hope is that Europa has lots of pure water."

"Isn't it *air* we're looking for?"

"Yes," he explains. "But water is actually made up of oxygen and hydrogen. Since the air we breathe contains a good percentage of oxygen as well as nitrogen, all we have to do is change the water into air."

"How will you do it?" you inquire.

"By taking a supply of pure water to Io. We'll use the heat from Io's volcanoes to transform the water into air."

"Sounds good to me," you reply.

Suddenly you see a glistening ball of light filling up the forward video screen.

"Is that Europa?" you ask.

"No doubt about it," replies Dr. Granville. "It's solid ice, but there may be water underneath."

"It looks so smooth and shiny," you say. "I thought there would be craters like there were on Callisto.

"Maybe fish live under the ice," you say. "Could we drill a hole and go fishing?"

"I've got a better idea," says Dr. Granville. "We could tie a rope to T.O.D. and have him swim under the ice."

"No thanks," says the android. "I don't want to get eaten by a giant fish."

"What kind of fish do you want to be eaten by, you metallic melon-head?" Dr. Granville asks.

"No kind of fish!"

You see that you're close enough to begin the landing procedure. T.O.D. gives you instructions. You begin slowing down the *Thunderbolt*.

As you get closer, you notice dark lines in the icy surface. "What are those?" you ask.

"Meteor scrapes," explains T.O.D. "If a meteor actually hits Europa, it will crash through the ice and the hole will freeze up again."

When you're only a thousand meters above the surface, you have a horrible thought. "What if *we* break through the ice?" you ask. "Maybe we shouldn't land here!"

"It's a little bit late to decide that, isn't it?"

"I guess so," you say nervously.

■ *To see how your landing turns out, turn to page 65.*

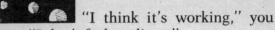

"I think it's working," you say. "I don't feel as dizzy."

"Good," replies Dr. Granville. "Now we can really breathe a sigh of relief."

You take a deep breath. "You bet!"

"We'd better head for home," says Dr. Granville. "Before something else goes wrong."

"But what about our mission?" you ask. "Shouldn't we explore the moons more carefully?"

"We've proved our point," the scientist explains. "By finding water, air, and fuel on the moons of Jupiter, we know that there are resources that can supply space colonies. Besides, I'm ready for a nice two-year nap, aren't you?"

You nod your head and when everybody is ready, you blast off into space. In your rearview screen, you see Io getting very small.

Then you see Jupiter behind it. You watch it turn majestically in the black star-filled sky.

After a few minutes, T.O.D. informs you

that the *Thunderbolt* has built up enough speed to fly back to Earth safely. Just as you open the Sonarest chamber, the cabin lights flicker. "What's wrong?" you shout.

"Oh, no!" cries Dr. Granville. "We should have hooked up the thermocouples back to the rocket engines. They power all the electrical systems in our ship."

"I'll put them back in now," says T.O.D.

"No, it's too dangerous," you say. "You could be blown off and drift into space."

"I'm only an android," replies T.O.D. "I'm expendable."

"Don't expend yourself before you put the thermocouples back," says Dr. Granville. "And be careful!"

"I thought you didn't care," the android says.

"Of course I don't care," snaps Dr. Granville. "I just don't want you to destroy the thermocouples or drop them into space."

"All right," says the android.

You watch as he goes out the air lock.

"I hope he makes it," you say.

"Don't ever tell him, but I hope so, too," says Dr. Granville. "I'd miss that rotten robot."

"I heard that!" says T.O.D.'s voice through the radio speaker.

"Shut up, you snoopy bag of silicon slime!" the scientist yells angrily.

"I think Dr. Granville likes you," you

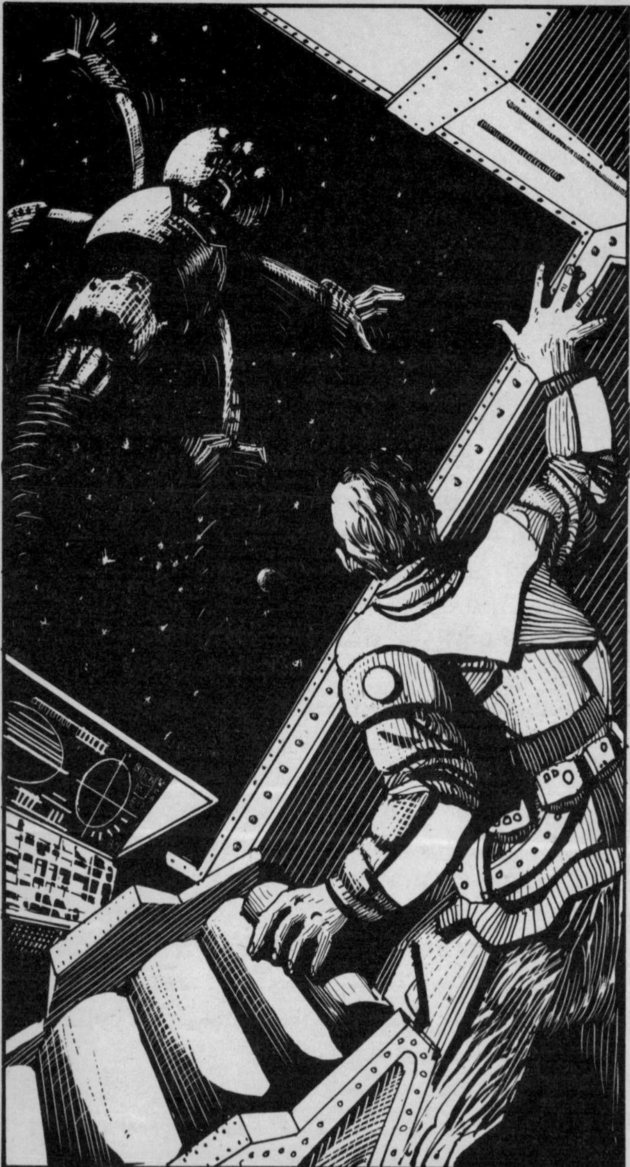

report to T.O.D. over the short-range radio that transmits from your ship to a tiny hand-held radio that the android's carrying. "He just can't admit it, that's all."

"Maybe he'll remember me fondly," replies T.O.D.

"What do you mean?"

"I just fell into the rocket exhaust."

"WHAT?" you shout.

"Don't worry," says the android. "I put the thermocouples back. Good-bye!"

You snap on the rear video screen. You can see T.O.D.'s form spinning through space away from the *Thunderbolt*.

Dr. Granville climbs back into the cabin. "What's all the excitement about? Isn't that robot coming back soon?"

"No!" you say. "He's falling toward Jupiter now."

"We've got to go back for him!" shouts Dr. Granville.

You look at T.O.D.'s tiny figure in the view screen.

"He risked his life for us. We can do no less for him," says Dr. Granville. "But you're the pilot, so you must make the final decision."

■ *Do you want to be safe and return to Earth now? Turn to page 104.*

■ *Do you want to try to rescue T.O.D.? Turn to page 88.*

You fly through space as fast as the *Thunderbolt* will go. There's not much air left and every second counts.

Suddenly you see a strange object up ahead. "Is there something wrong with our video screen?" you ask. "Does it need cleaning?"

"No, that's only Io," says Dr. Granville.

Io doesn't look like any of the other moons or planets you've seen. "Why is it so many different colors?" you mutter. "Red, orange, yellow, white, and black."

Dr. Granville smiles. "Io is probably the most mysterious object in the solar system. Unlike the rest of the moons and planets, Io is made mostly of sulfur."

"What are the other planets and moons made up of?" you ask.

"The inner planets, Mercury, Venus, Earth, and Mars, are made of various kinds of solid rocky materials such as iron, magnesium, calcium, and aluminum. The outer planets consist of ices such as water ice, ammonia ice, and methane ice."

"Whoa!" you shout. "Something just happened out in front of us. It looked like part of Io just splashed all over space. Should we turn back?"

"No," answers Dr. Granville. "Io is seething with volcanoes. They can eject sulfur over a hundred miles above the moon's surface. You'll have to be very careful to avoid them."

"*Now* you tell me," you say in amazement. You clutch the steering lever tightly. "I hope I can find someplace to land. Are you *sure* this is a good idea?"

"It's our only choice. Those sulfur volcanoes put out temperatures as high as six hundred degrees."

"I'll be careful," you promise. You head for a bright orange flat spot.

You take one last look at the strange surface below you. Then you cut the engines.

■ *Land on Io by turning to page 106.*

"I'm sorry, but we just can't risk it," you say. "We're heading back to Earth."

Dr. Granville looks very sad. "All right," he says reluctantly. "I'll abide by your decision."

Suddenly the radar alarm goes off. "What's that?" you ask, pointing to a large object on the screen. "How many moons does Jupiter have?"

"At least sixteen," replies the scientist. "I believe that's Pasiphaë up ahead."

"We're going to hit it unless I steer around it."

"So steer around it!"

You grab the control stick, and push it to the left. The spaceship responds by going into a looping roll. A funny thought crosses your mind. This is like being in one of those arcade games, only this is no game — this is for real!

The moon looms up in front of you. You try to level the spacecraft with the moon's surface, but it swoops and lurches wildly to the left, then to the right. Suddenly you realize what's wrong.

"Hey!" you shout. "This moon is going *backward*."

"I thought you knew," yells Dr. Granville. "Some of the outer moons of Jupiter orbit in the opposite direction of the inner moons."

"Why didn't anyone — "

CRASH!

THE END

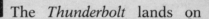

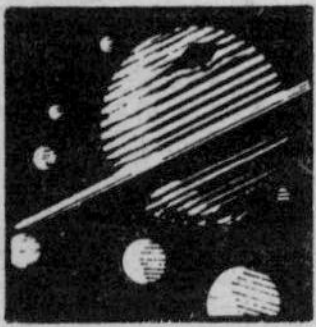

The *Thunderbolt* lands on Io . . . in one piece!

You quickly scan the ground below you on your remote control video camera. The surface is bright orange, but you see white patches on your left, red patches on your right, and the rim of a black volcano in front of you. "The ground seems solid. We were pretty lucky. Look at how high that volcano is shooting up into space!"

"Quick," says Dr. Granville. "We still have much work to do! We don't have time for sight-seeing. Our air is dangerously low. T.O.D., I want you to go outside."

"What for?"

"Inside our rocket tubes are the thermocouples."

"Oh, I get it," says the android. "You're going to use them to turn the water into air! Very clever."

"Thank you," Dr. Granville says, smiling proudly.

"I don't understand," you say. "What's a thermocouple?"

"They're electronic devices that turn

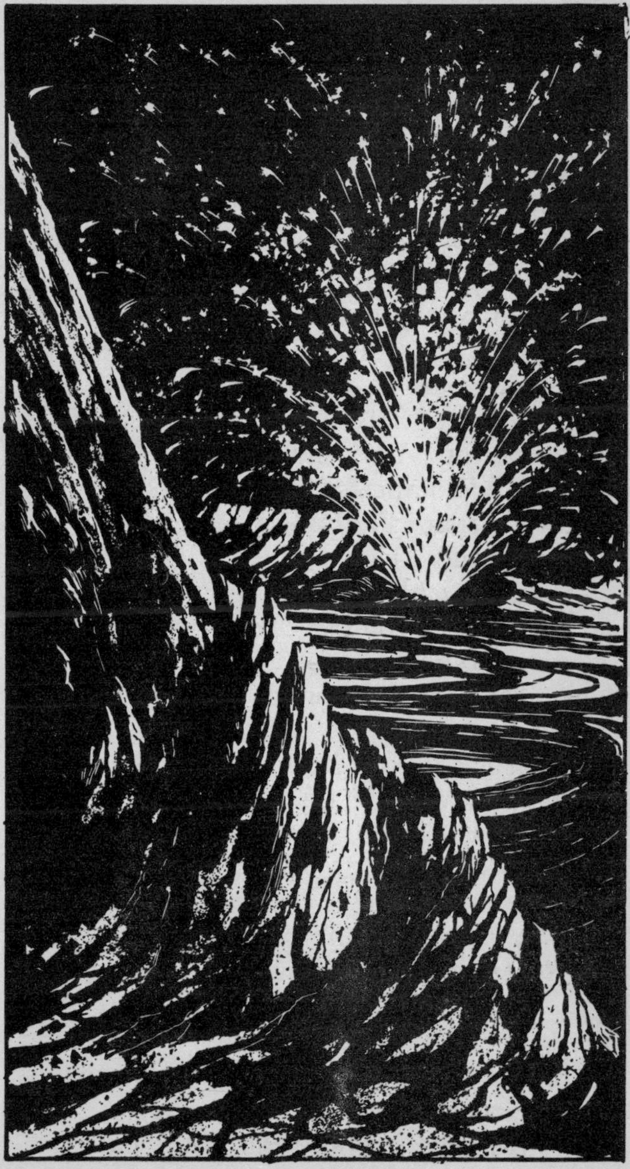

108

heat into electricity. We have them in the rocket motors so that we can get free electric power for the whole ship."

"But what does electricity have to do with changing water into air?"

"As I mentioned earlier, water is made up of oxygen and hydrogen. By passing an electric charge through water, you can break it up into the two gases."

"But why do I have to go outside and remove the thermocouples?" asks T.O.D.

"Because I'm telling you to, you cold-hearted computer!"

"No thanks!" the android replies. "*I'm* not going to risk my life. *You* remove the thermocouples."

"T.O.D.," you say, "Dr. Granville didn't mean to hurt your feelings."

"He doesn't have any feelings!" snaps Dr. Granville. "He's just a robot."

"How do you know I don't have feelings?" replies T.O.D.

"Now, T.O.D.," you say. "We all have to do our part. Dr. Granville will apologize, won't you?"

"Of course not," replies the scientist. "Not to a manipulating machine."

"All right, then *I'll* go out and remove the thermocouples," you say. "We're using up our oxygen by arguing when we should be working."

"All right," says T.O.D. "I'll go outside."

The android quickly races to the air lock. You and Dr. Granville go down to the storage hold.

You help the scientist assemble his equipment. Just as you finish, T.O.D. comes in with the thermocouples, pulling wires behind him. "Where do you want them?"

"You should have left the thermocouples outside and just brought in the wires," snaps the scientist. "My pocket calculator is smarter than you are."

"How was I supposed to know?" asks the android.

"T.O.D., take the thermocouples and put them into the nearest volcano. Connect the wires and trail them back here."

"You got it," answers the android.

You and Dr. Granville wait patiently. "I think it's getting stuffy in here," you say.

"It is," he says. "But we'll have plenty of air soon . . . I hope!"

Suddenly a pair of wires drops down from the hatch above your head. "I dumped the thermocouples in the volcano," the android calls down. "These wires are connected to them."

"I hope you hooked it up right, you bumbling bubble-head," grumbles Dr. Granville. He quickly ties the wires to the conversion chamber.

FZZZT!

Sparks jump!

"Is this safe?" you ask.

"No, but neither is running out of air," Dr. Granville replies.

You feel dizzy. "Are you sure this is working?" you ask.

"We'll know in a minute or two."

■ *To see if you'll have enough air, turn to page 98.*

You wake up from a dream about landing a spaceship on a giant pizza with sulfur volcanoes.

T.O.D. opens the green door of your Sonarest chamber.

"Are we back home?" you ask. "Is there any more trouble?"

"No," replies the android. "As soon as you're ready we can land."

"You don't have to ask me twice!" you cheer, jumping out of the chamber.

"I wasn't planning to," T.O.D. says.

You scramble up the ladder to the control room. "Wake up Dr. Granville, and I'll begin the landing procedure," you tell the android.

A few minutes later you're entering the atmosphere of planet Earth. Dr. Granville is beside you, and T.O.D. is leaning over your shoulder.

Watching the computer readouts, you keep your hand steady on the steering lever. You hold your breath the last few seconds.

Just before you hit the ground, you cut off the rocket motors.

WHUNK!

112

The ship wobbles. But only for a moment and then everything is absolutely quiet, except for the loud beating of your heart.

"Perfect!" cheers Dr. Granville. "You're getting pretty good at landings, old chum!"

You recognize the ISA headquarters on your video screen. Since your radio was smashed, no one expects you. But within moments, Josephine Fowler, ISA's president, rushes up to greet you. Earth's gravity is so strong that you're too weak to leave the ship for a few more minutes.

She introduces herself and extends her hand. "We were terribly concerned when we didn't hear from you. We're just so relieved you've gotten back safely."

"We've done it!" you tell her excitedly. "We've proved that humans can survive on the moons of Jupiter. Even though George Spiro destroyed our air, water, and fuel supplies, we were able to find substitutes on Io, Ganymede, and Europa."

"I can see the day when people will be living in space colonies on the moons of Jupiter," Dr. Granville remarks.

"There's plenty of room," you add.

ISA Security Guards come and take George Spiro away. "You've humiliated me again," he snarls at Dr. Granville.

"You did it to yourself," the scientist replies.

"I'll get you!" Spiro screams as the guards take him away.

"He could have been a hero, if he hadn't been so selfish," Dr. Granville says.

"*You* three are the greatest heroes the world has ever seen," says Ms. Fowler. "You risked your lives so that future generations can survive on Earth or in space. You'll receive a medal for this."

"I'd skip all the medals in the world," you tell her, "if I could bite into a big juicy hamburger."

"Right this way then," she says cheerily. "We'll give you a magnificent feast fit for an interplanetary appetite. After all, you haven't eaten in two years!"

"And we haven't had anything *decent* for four years," you add.

"What about me?" asks the android. "Don't I get anything special?"

The ISA president smiles. "We have a can of super-grade motor oil just for you, T.O.D."

THE END

114

TOP SECRET

1. Jupiter is the largest planet in the solar system, with a diameter of 88,900 miles. It is ten times bigger than Earth and ten times smaller than the Sun.

2. Jupiter and Earth both rotate around the Sun, but Jupiter's "year" (a trip around the Sun) is 12 times longer than our year. Jupiter is about 500,000,000 miles away from Earth.

3. A spaceship traveling at 31,000 miles an hour would take 23 months to get to Jupiter. Even a radio signal, traveling at the speed of light, would take almost an hour to travel between Earth and Jupiter.

4. Jupiter is not a solid planet like Earth — it consists mostly of hydrogen gas. Beneath Jupiter's clouds the gas is compressed to a slushlike "surface." But the air pressure there is a *million* times greater than the air pressure on Earth. And the temperature at that point would melt steel.

5. Jupiter also has a small set of narrow rings like its neighbor Saturn. The rings are made up of small particles of rock and dust and cannot be seen from Earth. Inside these rings is a belt of radiation that is deadly to human life.

6. Jupiter has 16 moons. Most of Jupiter's moons are small, averaging 10 to 20 miles across. Four of Jupiter's moons (Io, Europa, Ganymede, and Callisto) are very large, almost as big as planets.

7. Io is the fifth moon of Jupiter (counting outward). It is bright orange, yellow, white, and red. The bizarre colors come from blazing hot volcanoes that throw molten sulfur almost 200 miles above Io's surface.

8. Europa is the next moon out from Jupiter and is covered with a deep layer of smooth ice. Some scientists believe that deep beneath the ice is an ocean of liquid water.

9. Ganymede is the largest satellite of Jupiter. Its surface is a patchwork of ice, snow, soil, rock, and frozen organic materials.

10. Callisto is the last of the four giant moons of Jupiter. It is a world covered with craters, looking much like our own Moon. Its surface is made up of soil and ice, making it frozen mud.

END BRIEF.

■ *You are ready to return to your assignment. Turn to page 1.*

The Contributors

SETH MCEVOY has written seven Interplanetary Spy, six Not Quite Human, two Robo Force, and four Arcade Explorer books, the last with Laure Smith. In addition he has written three books about computers and a biography of science fiction author Samuel Delany. McEvoy is the author of Explorer #2, *Destination: Brain*.

WALTER P. MARTISHIUS is a book illustrator and theatrical set designer, and a production designer and art director for films. He is the illustrator of Time Machine #10, *American Revolutionary*, and of the Explorer series.